Kell

Macklins of Whiskey Bend, Book Four

Contemporary Western Romance

SHIRLEEN DAVIES

MACKLINS
OF WHISKEY BEND

Book Series by Shirleen Davies

Historical Western Romances

Redemption Mountain
MacLarens of Fire Mountain Historical
MacLarens of Boundary Mountain

Romantic Suspense

Eternal Brethren Military Romantic Suspense
Peregrine Bay Romantic Suspense

Contemporary Western Romance

MacLarens of Fire Mountain Contemporary
Macklins of Whiskey Bend

The best way to stay in touch is to subscribe to my newsletter. Go to my Website *www.shirleendavies.com* and fill in your email and name in the
Join My Newsletter boxes. That's it!

Avalanche Ranch Press, LLC
PO Box 12618
Prescott, AZ 86304

Book design and conversions by Joseph Murray at 3rdplanetpublishing.com

Cover design by Sweet 'n Spicy Designs

ISBN: 978-1-947680-67-8

I care about quality, so if you find something in error, please contact me via email at shirleen@shirleendavies.com

Description

**He's a warrior with a shattered future.
Will past mistakes prevent his accepting
the one woman who might mend his broken soul?**

Kellen Brooks is a broken man. Leaving his position in Special Forces three years earlier, he fought hard to build a new life and heal his damaged body. Working for his close friend, Boone Macklin, gives him purpose and a reason to focus on the future. Nothing else matters except soothing his wounded soul and reclaiming the family ranch.

Bethany Hutchison is determined to reach her goal of being accepted into law school. Working as a paralegal in a prestigious firm, combined with hours of classwork, takes all her time. Other than daily runs, nothing else could fit into her already packed schedule.

Kell's early morning runs on the high school track strengthen his recovering body and clear his mind. Nothing interferes with each day's goal, until a beautiful, leggy blonde sprints onto the track, stealing his breath.

As their fragile connection builds, an unexpected danger threatens to destroy whatever future they may have. Friends of Kell's are being targeted, and now the assailants are after Beth.

Kell, book four in the Macklins of Whiskey Bend Contemporary Western Romance series, is a stand-alone, full-length novel with an HEA and no cliffhanger.

Kell

Prologue

Location, South America

Army Ranger Staff Sergeant Kellen Brooks focused his binoculars on the MH-47 Chinook lifting off from the obscure field. It carried one of Kell's eight-man rifle squads and two rescued civilian hostages. The men of his second squad were covering the jungle around them, waiting for the bird to drop its load and return. If it had been his call, Kell would've loaded both squads in the Chinook, everyone leaving together.

Adjusting to look behind him, Kell studied the jungle between them and where they'd extracted their targets. Both men were safely aboard the Chinook, now a tiny dot on the horizon.

It had been textbook. Under the cover of a moonless night, two squads fast-roped into the dense jungle four miles on the south side of the terrorist compound. One squad provided cover while the second breached the complex and located the two hostages. They'd killed three tangos, losing none of their own, before meeting up with the other squad and taking a path north to their prearranged extraction point.

There'd been no shots, nothing to warn the terrorists of their quick entry and exit. The difficulty came from the hostages, both emaciated, with multiple wounds consistent with torture. They'd been in the confines of the compound for less than two weeks, yet it was apparent their stay had been brutal. The three mile trek required several unanticipated stops before reaching the extraction point.

With the hostages and several men in the air, Kell didn't allow himself or his remaining men to relax. All remained vigilant, their night vision goggles in place.

As the minutes passed, with no indication they'd been followed, the men chatted through the comms, releasing some of the adrenaline rush building from the moment they'd fast-roped to the ground.

"Cut the chatter. We aren't out of here yet." Kell's commanding voice stopped further comments.

"Movement at six o'clock, Sarge."

No sooner did the words come through the comms than bullets whizzed around them.

"I'm hit," one of his men ground out through the comms.

"I've got him, Sarge." But he didn't. The squad member took a bullet straight to his heart.

"Take cover and return fire!" Kell leveled his M4 carbine, fitted with an M203 grenade launcher, at the thick canopy of green. He fired several short bursts. Shifting, he did the same to his right. Screams confirmed he'd hit at least one of his targets.

"Foster's down, Sarge."

Kell's heart squeezed. "How bad?"

"He's gone, sir."

Kell's throat closed as he felt the loss of one of his closest friends. His gaze shot to Foster's last position. Dropping down, he crossed to the location, firing as he went.

Eyes fixed on the black sky, Foster had been felled by several shots to his chest. Knowing it was too late, Kell checked his pulse, cursing. He shoved thoughts of his friend's wife and children from his mind. There'd be time to grieve later.

Behind him, the distinctive whop-whop-whop of the Chinook signaled its return. Continuing to fire, Kell touched his earbud.

"Our ride is here. Move out. I'll take the rear. Don't leave anyone behind."

Providing cover, Kell grabbed Foster's pack, dragging his friend while firing at the tangos who'd killed him. Anger surged, but now wasn't the time to let it blur his thinking.

One of his men lumbered past him, a dead comrade slung over his back. Glancing behind him at the bird, Kell prayed the tangos didn't carry RPGs. The Chinook would be a perfect target for the rocket propelled grenades.

As the thought crossed his mind, an RPG hit the ground in front of the bird. Loading his M203 with a grenade, he aimed and fired. He repeated the action twice more, giving his men time to reach the Chinook while delaying additional RPGs from being fired.

"Come on, Sarge. We've got you covered." Kell gripped Foster's pack at Talbot's distinctive drawl.

Emerging from the cover of the jungle, Kell bent down, picking up Foster's body in a fireman's hold. Running, he kept his sights on the large Chinook and his men. They kept a steady barrage of gunfire trained past him. Talbot knelt on the floor of the Chinook, releasing two grenades into the thick forest.

"Load up," Kell shouted through the comms, his legs and back straining under the additional weight.

"Give him to me, Sarge." Talbot reached out, shifting Foster's body from Kell to the waiting bird. "Get in."

Grabbing onto Talbot's hand, Kell swung up, screaming in pain as a series of bullets hit him from behind. His grip loosened, body dropping to the ground.

Leaping to the ground, Talbot slung an arm around Kell, lifting, and all but throwing his sergeant into the Chinook while the remaining men provided cover. As the bird lifted, Talbot tossed his M4 inside, and jumped as bullets tore into his legs.

"Go!...Go!...Go!" Talbot croaked out the order before slipping into unconsciousness.

Chapter One

Whiskey Bend, Montana
Three years later...

Kell jogged onto the well-maintained high school track, picking up speed as he pounded forward. It didn't appear any different from when he and Boone Macklin had been eighteen, both believing nothing could stop them from achieving their dreams. At thirty, Kell knew how worthless dreaming could be.

Pain ripped through his legs and back, but he refused to slow down or stop. Today, he'd run seven miles, not his longest, but far more than he'd been able to do when arriving at the Macklin ranch in Whiskey Bend two years earlier.

Finishing mile three, Kell tried to stop his thoughts from going to the events of his last mission as an Army Ranger. The loss of a close friend and three other team members. Four men out of eight dead.

Of the four left alive, he and Zane Talbot were forced to choose between finishing their careers behind a desk or medical discharges. Both had chosen to leave.

The other two were still fighting PTSD, as well as injuries eliminating them from active duty as a Ranger.

They'd also chosen medical discharges over finishing their careers behind a desk.

Eight out of his eight man squad were dead or had left the service. Millions of dollars of training lost, along with some of the best men he'd had the honor to know.

If headquarters had taken Kell's suggestion to allow both squads to take the Chinook to base, everyone would've returned safely. The final call hadn't been his, a fact he still cursed three years later.

Completing mile five, Kell's mind slid over his work for the day. Most in Whiskey Bend saw him as a ranch hand for the Macklins. Basic labor at basement wages. Few knew his close friends had offered him a fifteen percent partnership, leaving Thorn and Del with twenty percent each, and Boone with forty-five.

As sheriff of Clayton County, Del spent as many Saturdays on the ranch as possible. Thorn, and his partners, owned Scorpion Custom Motorcycles. His time on the ranch mirrored Del's. On occasion, both brothers worked evenings and Sundays, taking their vacations to help.

Boone, the youngest Macklin, worked the ranch full-time. When their parents died in a plane crash, all three had been surprised to learn a hundred percent of the ranch had been left to him. A cruel joke from their hard-ass father who'd never forgiven Thorn or Del for pursuing their own dreams. It had taken Boone less than two weeks to present the percentage solution to his brothers.

Kell felt fortunate to be included at any amount. It was more than his own father had done.

Finishing mile six, he swiped sweat from his brow, deciding to extend the run to eight miles. Making the turn at one end of the field, his peripheral vision picked up a form entering the track.

Tank top, skimpy running shorts, long, lean legs, and a blonde ponytail swinging with each step. Kell had seen her one other time, hoping she'd return.

Slowing his pace, he allowed her to pass him, not wanting to miss the view. As before, something about the woman tickled his memory. It should be easy to recall where he'd seen a beautiful woman. Not this one.

Coming up on his eighth mile, Kell slowed, feeling both a heaviness in his chest and deep satisfaction. He'd walk for five minutes before heading back to the ranch.

Today would be busy. Four mares were ready to foal. Buyers were already confirmed, deposits in the bank. Their work was far from over. The agreement with the buyers included two years of boarding and training, with no restriction on how often the owners visited.

Taking one last look at the woman who still ate up the track, he walked to his truck. Kell couldn't stop a grin each time he spotted the gunmetal gray vehicle purchased a few months earlier.

Grabbing a towel, he wiped away the moisture before tossing it aside to answer his phone.

"Yeah."

"Kell, it's Maggie O'Dell."

"I'll bet you're calling about the mare's progress."

The thirtyish woman called every day, sometimes twice. A widow with a young girl, she worked long hours as a detective with the Whiskey Bend Police Department. When necessary, she partnered with his friend, Detective Rick Zoeller.

"Well, yes. My daughter is crazy excited. She's begging me to bring her by the ranch. Would today be convenient?"

"Anytime after ten." Climbing behind the wheel, he pulled onto the street. "I'm in town and have a few stops to make."

"How about one this afternoon?"

"Works for me. I'll see you then."

Dropping the phone beside him, he thought of Maggie. Petite with a girl-next-door appearance, you wouldn't know she could take down a two-hundred pound man with little effort. He'd thought about asking her out, deciding to hold off until after the mare gave birth. Boone razzed him, saying his waiting had nothing to do with the foal and everything to do with getting back in the saddle. Kell couldn't argue.

Dating hadn't been a part of his life since before the mission in South America. Healing from the extensive wounds, physical therapy, psych evaluations, and a short stint on desk duty, took up most of his time for the first year. When he'd been denied a return to active duty, the next two years had been spent at the ranch, getting his head straight. If anyone asked him a few years ago if he'd go over three years without a woman, he would've laughed. He didn't laugh about his lack of companionship anymore.

Each shower reminded him of the disfiguring scars on his legs and back. Some caused by bullets, some from numerous surgeries. He'd never thought himself vain, and his reticence about meeting women shamed him.

Thorn gave him hell, telling him men with far more severe wounds met women, dated, and married. Kell knew his friend was right. It was time to do more than spend weekends working, fishing, hunting, running the track, or stretching out with a beer. Maggie might be the perfect person to help him resurrect a social life.

Parking in the feed store lot, the ringing phone drew his attention. His lips twitched at the phone number. "Yeah."

"Sorry to bother you again, but would two o'clock be all right?"

"Anytime this afternoon is fine, Maggie."

"Good. See you at two."

Yep, Maggie might be just the person to save him from the rut he'd settled into.

"There's a call for you, Beth."

Bethany Hutchison removed her glasses, rubbing her eyes before picking up the phone. "This is Beth."

"Hey."

Wincing, she leaned back in the chair, not ready for this conversation. "Hello, Mick."

"You sound tired."

"Not really. There's a heavy caseload right now. It'll smooth out in a week or so."

At least she hoped it would. She'd been hired as a legal assistant four months earlier, moving from Billings, Montana, after ending a toxic relationship. She had no interest in Mick, or any other man.

"How about having dinner with me tonight? It'll take your mind off work."

"Can't. I already have plans." Hot bath, glass of wine, and finishing a paper for her constitutional law class. One and a half years to go for her undergraduate degree. She was already taking practice LSAT exams for entry into law school.

"Tomorrow then."

Beth had made the mistake of accepting a lunch invitation from Mick not long after arriving in Whiskey Bend. The man refused to accept she held no interest in him.

"I've already been told to plan to work late at the office." Standing, she looked over the top of the divider which separated her space from the receptionist. Alana had been with the firm since high school. She and Beth had become fast friends.

"I'd better go, Mick. Enjoy your day." Ending the call, she dropped into her chair, letting out a pent-up breath.

She couldn't afford to be rude. Whiskey Bend was too small to burn any bridges, and Mick too well-respected.

"Sorry for putting the call through, Beth." Alana stood outside the cubicle, her gaze moving around the office. "Mr. Lawson walked up just when I answered the phone."

"No worries. Mick is persistent."

"And he wants you to quit here to work for him."

"Which won't happen. Lawson and Chapman is the best firm between here and Missoula. Besides, the thought of working with Mick...well...I can't imagine."

"Someone just walked in. Talk later."

Stretching arms above her head, Beth eyed the stack of folders, each one a project for either Lawson or Chapman. Larry Lawson founded the firm twenty years ago after practicing at a large Missoula firm. Janet Chapman earned a partner spot ten years later. The two were a powerhouse of legal and business knowledge.

Five years from now, Beth hoped to be hired as a junior attorney, someday earning a partnership. She already knew her specialties. Estate and family law, both areas had held her interest since high school. If anyone asked why, Beth didn't know if she could give a convincing answer.

Most of her interest came from having friends whose parents divorced. There were horror stories of men, and some women, losing everything in spousal and child support when the split wasn't their idea. Everything they'd worked for went to their former spouse, leaving them to make do with whatever they could afford. It had happened to her best friend.

When her father discovered her mother's affair, she filed for divorce. The judge awarded her the bulk of their savings, the house, and ordered spousal support be paid to her, even though she made more than her husband.

Beth's friend refused to see or talk to her mother again, choosing to live with her father in a tiny two-bedroom apartment. There were other stories with disastrous legal rulings which ruined people's lives. Although she had no idea how, Beth hoped to bring some sanity to family law.

Janet Chapman warned her to be open-minded during law school, and not be too focused on one specialty. Beth promised she would.

Picking up a file, she read through Janet's instructions before scanning the documents. Six hours later, she closed the last file, adding it to the stack of completed work. She'd deliver them to the appropriate attorney before leaving.

Beth thought of her early morning run at the high school, and the man who came every morning. She'd recognized him her first time on the track.

Kell Brooks. She'd thought of him many times since meeting at the Macklin ranch while visiting her cousin, Sarah Mae. She'd been out of character that evening, wearing clothes more suitable for clubbing than a country evening on the porch.

Kell had been distant, wrestling with something he didn't share. She'd felt for him, wished there'd been something she could do. There wasn't.

Other feelings had taken hold that evening. Emotions Beth hadn't felt before or since. A primal desire for the struggling soldier.

Spotting him on the high school track had been unexpected. Kell was the reason she'd adjusted her schedule for several weeks, showing up right after he'd driven away. This morning, Beth had decided she owed herself some eye candy, and Kell Brooks fit the description.

Someday, she might even build up the nerve to reintroduce herself. For now, it was enough to run on the same track each morning and fantasize about the man who checked all her boxes.

Chapter Two

"Mommy, Mommy, come see." Six-year-old Ashley O'Dell tugged on her mother's hand, trying to drag her to one of two large stalls used for birthing. "I think the baby is coming now."

Maggie smiled at Kell. "Are you coming?"

"Sure am. Don't want to miss the baby entering the world."

Maggie chuckled at his reference to a baby instead of a foal. She bet he heard everything from Macklin ranch clients, especially the young ones.

Following behind, he checked his phone's battery. Kell made it a point to take pictures whenever clients visited for special events, such as a mare giving birth. Although ninety percent sure Patsy wouldn't present them with a foal this afternoon, he didn't want to spoil Ashley's excitement.

Boone and Thorn were at an auction in Billings. Del was attending a trial in Missoula regarding a drug bust his department assisted with. Kell had a good deal of experience with birthing from his time here and at his family's ranch a couple miles up the road. Or what had been the family ranch before his father cut Kell out of it. The action still felt bitter in his mouth. Knowing his son wanted to buy it, his father sold the entire two thousand acres while Kell fought overseas. The two men hadn't spoken since Kell learned about his father's betrayal.

As Boone's wife, Willow, said more than once, the sale and the loss of his men in South America were part of his past. His future was still to be written.

"Come on, Kell. You're going to miss it."

Smiling at Ashley's enthusiasm, he jogged after them, a rare smile lifting the corners of his mouth. Entering the barn, he spotted Patsy standing in the birthing stall, eating from the feeder attached to the metal rails at the front.

From her stance, and the fact she wasn't pacing or circling to ready a place to lay down, he knew the mare had a day or more to go. It wouldn't surprise him if Maggie and Ashley were back at the ranch tomorrow. Patsy was that close.

"Does her big belly hurt?" Ashley bounced on the balls of her feet, both hands wrapped around the metal rails.

"Can't say for sure, but I doubt it's comfortable. One thing about Patsy, the old girl never complains."

Ashley looked at him, brows scrunching. "Does she talk?"

Maggie placed a hand on her daughter's shoulder. "Of course she doesn't. Kell was making a joke."

Looking at the ground, then him, she giggled. "Funny."

Resting his arms on the top rail, Kell studied the mare. Patsy had birthed eight foals in her lifetime. Boone thought she might have two to three more before retiring to become a beginner's riding horse.

"When can I ride, Mommy? You said I could after my sixth birthday. I am six, you know."

"Yes, sweetheart. I know. Let's get through this with Patsy, then we'll figure something out."

"Promise?"

Seeing the hesitation on Maggie's face, Kell stepped closer to Ashley. "You want to see something pretty exciting?"

Grinning, she jumped up and down. "Yes!"

Walking toward the open doorway, he motioned for her to follow. "This way."

Skipping behind him, Ashley glanced over her shoulder to see Maggie a few feet away. Hurrying to catch up to Kell, she came to a stop around the corner of the house and gasped.

"Puppies!" Rushing forward, she knelt down, eyes wide. "One, two, three, four, five, six puppies. Can I hold one?"

"Ashley?"

She looked at her mother, then back at Kell. "Please can I hold one?"

"If you're careful. Let me help you." Looking at the puppies, he selected a sturdy male with brown fur. Scooping him up, Kell laid the whining pup in Ashley's cupped hands.

"He's so soft." Giggling, her fingers stroked the fur. She giggled again when the pup squirmed, licking her hands.

Kell's gaze moved from Ashley to Maggie, watching her reaction. He knew they didn't have any pets. Not since their dog was killed, along with her husband when he lost control on a slick, icy road, rolled down an embankment, crashing into a tree. It had been three years. Maggie still struggled with the loss of the man she'd loved since high school.

"Can I have one, Mommy?"

"I'd have to think about it, honey."

"I'll take care of him. He can stay in my room. Please..."

Kell could see the struggle on Maggie's face. "I'll think about it. Now give the puppy back to Kell. We have twenty minutes to get you to your gymnastics class."

"I don't want to go."

"Ashley, hand the puppy back."

"But..."

Kell held out his hand. "Hand him to me so he can join his brothers and sisters."

After a long sigh, Ashley did as he asked, watching as he set the puppy in the large cage.

"Can I see him again?"

Kell shot a look at Maggie. "It's up to your mom."

Resigned, she nodded. "You can see them the next time we visit the ranch."

Jumping up, Ashley's features changed from disappointment to joy in a heartbeat. "Okay."

Kell and Maggie lagged behind as Ashley ran toward their car. "My schedule doesn't allow room for a pet," she defended. "I already work fifty hours a week."

"You don't have to explain. Being a single parent is a lot of work. I watched Boone with Tyler before he married Willow. Don't know how he did it."

"He adopted Tyler, didn't he?"

Kell stopped several feet from her car. "Ty's mother died of cancer. There was no one to take her son. No family, and few close friends. Boone stepped up. It's been over three years, and no one would guess he's not the birth father."

"Hurry up, Mommy. I'll be late."

Maggie offered a wan smile. "Better get a move on. Thanks for letting us visit, Kell."

"Anytime. Give me a call and I'll make it happen."

Shoving hands into his pockets, he watched them navigate the drive back to the county road. As much as he wanted to spend time with Maggie, get to know her, she wasn't ready. Some people moved on from tragedy sooner than others. A few never accepted the loss. He didn't know how long it would take her, but Maggie still grieved. The same as he still grieved the loss of Kyle Foster and the others in his squad.

Refusing to allow himself to dwell on the past, Kell headed to the pasture behind the barn. Stopping at the sound of a vehicle, he turned to see Cody approach in the dark blue Chevy truck his parents gave him for his sixteenth birthday. Twenty years old and requiring a good deal of TLC, Cody couldn't be more proud of his ride. Three days a week and Saturdays, the high schooler worked on the ranch. A good worker with a great attitude, Kell welcomed his help.

"Hey, Cody. The truck looks good."

The tall, lanky, high school junior stepped out, beaming at Kell's praise. "I clayed and waxed her yesterday. Dad helped me install a new stereo system over the weekend. She's sounding great."

"I'll bet she does."

Pocketing the keys, Cody glanced behind Kell to the barn. "Where do you want me to start?"

"I need to check the fences close to the house. I'd like you to stick close, keep watch on the mares. The one in the birthing stall is close. Might be tonight."

Cody's eyes brightened. "Hope I'm here."

"Hay needs to be moved from the stackyard to the barn. A dozen bales should be enough for now. There's also a few broken rails in the pasture behind the barn."

"I'll take care of them, Kell. An outside faucet is leaking. Shouldn't take much to fix it."

"I should be back by the time you're done." Heading to the pasture, Kell whistled for his gelding, Joker.

The horse he'd owned since fifteen died while he'd been deployed, a year before the disaster in South America. About the same time his father had sold the family ranch. Kell remembered the double punch to his gut in the same letter from his mother. His dad hadn't had the guts to explain his actions.

19

Joker had been a gift from the Macklins when he showed up after his medical discharge. The chestnut quarter horse measured sixteen hands, showing a white blaze and socks. At six, Joker had been well trained for work on the ranch. Kell knew the brothers could've gotten three thousand for Joker. Refusing to accept the horse outright, the men had settled on Kell paying fifteen hundred, the rest being a gift.

Tacking up the gelding, he rode east about a mile toward the Bitterroot Mountains. Following the fence line, he stopped several times to check the wire, tightening or repairing a few spots.

Kell relished the solitude, even turning off his phone. Drawing in a deep breath, he exhaled, feeling his body relax.

Slowing his pace, he thought of the woman at the track that morning. Her long, lean body, arms pumping in sync with her legs. Sunglasses hid her features. Still, he had the strangest sense they'd met.

The feed store? He shook his head. Wicked Waters Saloon? He dismissed the thought. The bank? He almost never went inside. Nothing triggered an answer.

She appeared young, years behind him, indicating they hadn't attended Whiskey Bend High School at the same time. Maybe she'd been in the doctor's or dentist's office the same time as him. Had he met her in the grocery store? He rarely struck up conversations with fellow shoppers. In and out, not lingering or deviating from the short list on his phone.

Long, blonde hair, and skin tanned from the sun, not from a booth in one of the tanning salons in Missoula. Kell guessed her to be five feet seven or eight, but she could be taller. Unlike most women who garnered his attention, she wasn't curvaceous, which puzzled him. He didn't usually go for the lean, athletic type.

Scrubbing a hand down his face, Kell chided himself. It had been so long since being with a woman, he didn't know if he still had a type. All he knew was the lady intrigued him.

Dismounting, he studied a break in the four-strand barbed wire. Not a break, but a clean cut.

"What the hell?"

Pulling out his phone, he took a few pictures. Several clipped wires made sense if someone wanted to steal Macklin cattle, or their prized horses.

Grabbing a piece of two and a half mil fencing wire and fencing pliers from his saddlebags, he made a quick repair, intending to return tomorrow on the ATV for a more permanent fix. The job took little time. Straightening, he stood back, still puzzled by the clean cut. Using his phone, Kell took note of the exact coordinates for when he returned.

Something in the bushes fifty yards away caught his attention. A glint of sunshine on metal. His gut tightened. For a moment, he dismissed the sight as nothing more than an aluminum can. Then the flash came again.

He dropped to his belly as a bullet whizzed over his head. Lying flat, he reached behind him to the holster he

21

often wore while riding. Sliding out his Ruger Blackhawk .44 mag, Kell raised his head to look around.

The sound of an engine starting, tires spinning on the dirt, and a dust cloud in the distance, indicated whoever fired the shot was gone. He kept his position for five minutes before standing.

Holding the gun at his side, he made a slow turn, not expecting to see anyone. Holstering the Blackhawk, he mounted Joker, riding to the spot where he saw the flash of metal. Pushing through the brush, he came to a clearing accessed by a dirt road.

With one shot, he figured there'd be no spent shell, but he walked the area to make sure. For ten minutes, he searched, finding nothing to help him figure out who fired into the pasture.

Chapter Three

"It had to be teenagers." Kell spooned a second scoop of mashed potatoes onto his plate, not satisfied with what he'd said.

"Whoever fired the shot had to have seen you and Joker." Boone's expression indicated the extent of his anger at his friend being targeted. "It wasn't an accident."

Boone's wife, Willow, placed a slice of meatloaf on Tyler's plate, her mind on what happened in the pasture. "I have to agree with Boone. There's one way in and out of the dirt road. It's not hunting season, and there are signs posted. It worries me."

"Same here. I'm going to ask Del to come out and get his opinion." Chewing a scoop of potatoes with the meatloaf, Boone smile. "This is great, Willow."

Kell leaned back in his chair. "There's no sense dragging Del into this. He's got enough to do with the recent hit on two convenience stores."

"Thorn's shop also was broken into. Probably unrelated," Boone said. "Del's got deputies to work those incidents. He'll be out tomorrow to help with some work around the ranch. Might as well have him check the area."

"Del needs to know about it, Kell." Willow's voice was gentle, yet firm.

Arguing would be useless. When Willow agreed with her husband, the decision wouldn't change.

Setting down his fork, Boone stared at the remaining meatloaf, wrestling with having a third helping. "Anyone have a problem with you?"

Kell snorted a chuckle. "The list is long and distinguished."

"Can I go check on the puppies, Mom? I finished my dinner."

Tyler's use of mom still had her chest squeezing. Losing his mother at six had been hard on him. Without the adoption, Tyler would've entered the foster system. Within days of Willow and Boone marrying, he'd started calling her mom.

"All right, but just the pups."

Shoving back his chair, Tyler took a step away before Boone's words stopped him. "Don't go anywhere else without getting one of us." He nodded at Willow and Kell.

"Okay." With that, he tore through the kitchen and out the door.

"After what happened in the pasture, I'm not taking any chances." Picking up his cup, Boone sipped the cooling coffee. "Although you're probably right. Might've just been a teenager not paying attention."

Kell hoped so, yet his instincts warned him otherwise. He'd be making calls and doing research after dinner.

Willow didn't notice Kell's growing unease, her thoughts were focused on the impending addition to the Macklin family. Looking down at her growing stomach, she shot a look at her husband, who offered a knowing expression. After the shared tragedy of their past, the couple grew more cautious as the delivery date approached.

"How are you feeling, sweetheart?" Reaching out, Boone took her hand in his.

"Great. The walks are helping."

"Then we'll take one tonight. Ty can go with us." Standing, Boone began picking up plates. Kell did the same, joining him in the kitchen. Confirming Willow hadn't left the table, he lowered his voice.

"Maybe I should move out for a while."

Setting down the plates, Boone rested both hands on the kitchen counter. "Not a chance. We know nothing about the circumstances. Plus, it happened during the day. You moving out wouldn't change anything."

Boone's words rolled around in Kell's head as he finished his last call. The conversation bothered and angered him. Wondering why no one had bothered to notify him of one of his former teammate's death a few weeks earlier, he initiated an internet search. Less than a minute later, he scanned the initial article, moving to the obituary. He read aloud.

"Robert Brian Moser, twenty-seven, was pronounced dead at the scene after a severe crash on CR 183. Deputies speculated Mr. Moser lost control of his vehicle, rolled down an embankment, smashing into a concrete cistern.

The presence of drugs or alcohol has not been determined."

The calls Kell made confirmed there'd been both alcohol and opioids in his system. It made no sense.

The obituary mentioned Moser's parents and sister, and the address for donations to an organization working with vets suffering from PTSD. Kell wrote down the information. A check would be sent tomorrow, along with a card.

As Moser's former sergeant, he'd known a good deal about the man, and the diagnosis of PTSD after the events in South America. The last time Kell had spoken with Brian, he'd been doing well, had landed a job as a security specialist for a local tech company in his hometown of Austin, Texas.

Scrubbing hands down his face, Kell closed his computer. He checked the time. Nine o'clock. Still early enough to call Cliff Walker, another of the South American survivors. Dialing, he waited. One...two...three...until Cliff's voice came on, asking to leave a message.

"Cliff, it's Kell. Call me."

One left. Zane Talbot had saved Kell's life, providing cover before hauling him into the Chinook. Each received career ending wounds to their backs and legs, but they were alive.

Punching Zane's number into his phone, Kell waited. His friend worked for an online game company in Irvine, California, a place Kell knew Zane hated.

SoCal, with its crowded cities, smog, miles of homeless, and restrictive regulations, didn't appeal to a man who'd grown up near Bozeman before joining the Army. The offer from the game company had been too good to pass up. Zane now sat in one of the unending cubicles, providing real world experience to employees creating games based on true life military battles.

"This couldn't be Staff Sergeant Kellen Brooks. I heard he spends all his time shoveling shit, and hauling hay."

"You wish your ass was outside instead of warming a seat next to teenagers, ground pounder."

"Hell, don't I know it. How ya doing, Kell?"

"Good. I'm running every morning. Pushing for nine miles. Back is good, and I'm mostly off the meds. You?"

"Shoulder's doing fine. Still on PT once a week, but that'll end in another month. My head's straight, which pleases my mom. Dad doesn't care one way or another."

Kell knew that for the lie it was. "Firefighter, right?"

"Just retired as chief in a town near Bozeman. He's getting a darn good retirement check each month. Maybe I should've gone that direction."

"The same as I should've stayed on the ranch." Kell rubbed the back of his neck.

"We made our choices."

"Do you ever think about going home?"

Zane hesitated a moment. "Back to Montana? All the time. I'd have to first figure out how to make a living."

"You worked on your family's ranch, right?"

"Right. Remember, it's a small spread. Two hundred acres is all. More a working farm with horses. With my dad working at the fire station, it was Mom and me keeping it together much of the time. By the time I left, Dad made enough money to hire part-time help. I wouldn't have left if it meant Mom doing most all the work. With him retired, they work together."

"Come to Whiskey Bend. We'll be looking to hire in another few months. The sheriff, Del Macklin, has an opening for a deputy. I could get you an interview."

"No more guns for me, Kell. Not unless I'm hunting or shooting rattlers. Anyway, I'd probably be DQ'd because of my shoulder."

"Send me your most recent medical report and I'll show it to Del."

"I'll think about it."

"There's another reason I called, Zane. Did you hear about Brian Moser?"

"No. What happened?"

"Ran off the road. Rolled his truck and slammed into a concrete cistern. He's dead, Zane."

The spew of expletives didn't surprise Kell. Brian was well-liked and a hell of a Ranger. "Services were a couple weeks ago. I just heard about it myself. I called around. The coroner's report said he was full of alcohol and opioids."

"Not a chance, Kell. He didn't drink, and unless it was prescribed, didn't take drugs. Not even an aspirin."

"I couldn't reach Cliff. Have you spoken to him recently?"

"It's been a few months." Zane quieted for a moment before his voice lowered. "He didn't sound good. PT wasn't helping his leg, plus he's not working. No family, few friends. Look, I've gotta go. Let's talk in a few days. I'll try to reach Cliff."

"Later, man. Watch your back."

None of what Zane said had Kell feeling better. He made a mental note to call Cliff until he got through, and check with Zane more often. The bitter taste in his mouth hadn't lessened. Instead, it was as strong as ever.

Beth pounded the hard dirt, glad for the heavy cloud cover. The prediction of rain hadn't happened...yet. She'd be real glad if the storm held off for another hour.

Taking a quick glance around, her heartbeat ratcheted up. Kell stood by the gate, watching her. She'd sworn off men, but this man did something to her insides, which made her want to rethink the self-restraint. Remembering to breathe, Beth forced herself to concentrate on running.

Making the long turn at one end, she spotted him out of the corner of her eye. He seemed to be having some trouble with one leg. Not wanting to stare, she checked the time. Five more minutes and she'd be heading out.

Footfalls behind her had Beth slowing. There was no way he could've caught her, yet there he was, not ten paces behind. A mischievous grin appeared as he began to pass.

"Showoff."

Deep, rich laughter burst from him, slowing his progress. Turning around, he continued to run backward, the most amazing smile she'd seen in ages focused on her. This time, she was the one to laugh.

Moving off the track, she watched another minute before heading to her small SUV for a towel and water. With each step, she forced herself not to look over shoulder. Beth didn't believe he'd appreciate her watching him. Even the thought had her face heating up.

"Do I know you?"

Jumping, she whirled around. "Geez. Give a girl some warning."

He continued to watch her, the devastating smile still in place. "Thought you'd hear me coming."

"Yeah, well...my mind was elsewhere."

"Ah. Anyway, you look familiar."

Beth felt a strange pull toward him, an impulse to reach out and touch him. She was going to need a real cold shower.

"You're Kell Brooks."

Eyes narrowing, he crossed his arms, the playfulness fading.

"I doubt you'll remember me. We met a few years ago. I'm Bethany Hutchison."

Brows scrunching, his gaze moved over her, as if dissecting every inch. "Bethany?"

"My cousin is Sarah Mae. My friends call me Beth."

As a memory flashed through him, Kell took a step away. "You're the same girl who was with Sarah Mae at the ranch?"

"Strange, I know. Not how I usually dress. Anyway, it's good to see you again. I need to get ready for work, so..."

"Where do you work?"

"Lawson and Chapman. It's a law firm—"

"I know who they are. Larry Lawson took care of my parents' legal issues before they moved to Florida. I've done some work with him." His tone made it clear the experience hadn't gone well.

"I'm a legal assistant, trying to finish my degree to attend law school."

Kell said nothing for a long moment before turning to leave. "Good luck, Bethany Hutchison."

Chapter Four

Bethany tapped a pencil on the pad in front of her, struggling with what she wanted to do versus what she should do, which was stay quiet. Her work was complete, the office would close in five minutes, yet she sat rooted to her chair.

"Miss Hutchison, do you have a minute?"

"Of course, Mr. Lawson."

"Bring your pad, please."

The case he wanted to discuss didn't take long, leaving her with a decision. "Do you mind if I ask a question, Mr. Lawson? It's not about this case."

"Is it about an existing client?"

"Yes, sir."

Standing, Larry walked around his desk, leaning against the edge. "Go ahead."

"Kellen Brooks."

Tipping his head back, Larry looked at the ceiling for so long Bethany didn't think he'd answer. Lowering his head, his features told her nothing.

"Kell is one of the best men I've had the pleasure to know. He gave a lot for his country, works hard, and is loyal. Unfortunately, he came from a man who had none of those qualities. Worse, that man was my client and made decisions I can't discuss. I will say they affected Kell poorly."

She sat still for several moments, waiting...for what, she didn't know.

"I take it you've met Kell."

"Yes, sir."

"He mentioned me."

"Not in so many words, sir. He asked where I worked. The answer obviously bothered him. It doesn't really matter, we're barely acquaintances. It's doubtful I'll see him again."

Standing, she walked to the door.

"Miss Hutchison."

"Yes, sir?"

"He's worth getting to know."

Kell sliced through another log, tossing the pieces into the growing pile, sweat rolling off his naked torso. His arms, legs, and back were screaming at him to rest. Kell ignored the pain, choosing to continue the brutal physical work. The more often he swung the blade, the less his thoughts would linger on the beautiful runner.

He couldn't believe his luck. Not only was Bethany the woman who'd hung out at the ranch one night during his final leave, but she worked for Larry Lawson.

The senior partner at Lawson and Chapman. The man who'd allowed Kell's father to sell the ranch out from under him. The deal had been airtight. By the time Kell learned of the sale, there wasn't one thing he could do to reverse it. The family legacy had been lost, his father uncaring he'd broken a promise to his son.

At least he didn't have to see either his father or Larry again. Kell did one brief transaction with the legal whiz after returning to the Macklin ranch. Additional legal work would be accomplished outside the biggest law firm in Whiskey Bend.

Resting the ax against the cutting block, he drained two bottles of water, recalling what he'd heard at Robinson's Feed and Tack. As the owner, Willow spoke with as many customers as time would allow. Kell had overheard her speaking with the new owner of what should've been his ranch. From what he'd heard, Jim Jernigan was running out of money.

No surprise to Kell. Jim and his wife, Connie, had purchased the acreage and house to start over after a venture capital firm took control of the company where he worked. He'd been one of two hundred laid off. Neither had experience on a ranch or farm. Jim implied to Willow they might be open to selling some of the acreage.

Kell made the decision to bide his time, say nothing to Willow about what he'd overheard. A meeting with the bank manager, a friend who'd gone to high school with him and Boone, determined the money required to buy the ranch at different acreages.

Grasping an eighteen inch log, he placed it on the block before raising the ax. Working for another twenty minutes, he didn't slow when Boone walked within a few feet of the cut pile. Crossing his arms, Boone watched his friend for a few minutes.

"Something bothering you, Kell?"

"No."

"Don't believe we've ever had a stack of cut wood this large."

Kell didn't respond until he'd thrown the last pieces on the pile. "It's done." Grabbing his shirt, he wiped down his face and neck before slipping it on. "I can use a wheelbarrow to stack them up wherever you want."

"Leave it. We've got several months before the cold weather sets in. Let's go inside. We'll have coffee, and you can tell me what's going through your head."

Following, Kell sorted through what he'd tell Boone. Bethany was off the table. The rifle shot yesterday and his meeting at the bank were his choices. Perhaps choosing wouldn't be needed.

Boone set two cups of black coffee on the table, sliding one toward Kell. "Del walked the area outside the pasture where the shot came from. He didn't find anything. Noting the posted No Trespassing signs, and the fact whoever fired couldn't have missed spotting you and Joker, Del doesn't believe the shot was an accident."

Leaning forward to rest his arms on the table, Kell's jaw drew tight. "Not an accident."

"Del believes whoever fired at you may try again. There's no way to know. He is going to have deputies patrol the roads leading onto our property."

Meeting Boone's gaze, Kell gave a slow, contemplative nod. "There has to be at least five entry spots, plus the driveway. He doesn't have enough people to keep watch on all of them."

"He suggested putting up cameras at each spot. I wrote down the manufacturer, but Del's going to order what we need."

"I'll pay you back."

"Not going to happen." Boone lifted his cup, taking a long swallow of coffee.

"It's because of me you're installing cameras."

"Thorn, Del, and I discussed cameras over a year ago. Thorn thought it a good idea to have eyes on the horses located in the corrals close in. We decided to order some, but disagreed about where they should be installed. There are now six locations which make sense. It's a good place to start. Del's going to order a dozen."

"I'll pay my share, the same as the rest of you." Kell knew the Macklins couldn't argue the point. Not with him owning fifteen percent of the ranch. "It's too soon for me to round up my guys."

Boone knew he meant men who'd been in his squads over the years. "And Del could be wrong. The shooter could be long gone by now. Scaring you might've been his goal."

"I'm not scared. Just mad." Standing, he picked up the coffeepot, refilling each of their cups. "There's something else I want to run past you."

"Does it have to do with the shooting?"

36

Lowering himself back onto the chair, Kell shook his head. "Nope. Has to do with the people who bought my family's ranch."

The Macklins, and most long timers, knew about Kell's dream of taking over some day. He'd even spoken with the bank manager before leaving on the last mission, told his father of how it could work. Kell's father had agreed to hold off selling to anyone else until his son returned.

"The word is the Jernigans are experiencing financial troubles. Might need to sell some acreage."

"Willow mentioned the same. She spoke with Jim when he came into the feed store. You're interested in buying?"

"Depends on how many acres. Would you boys be interested in doing a partnership?"

One corner of Boone's mouth turned upward. "Absolutely. If you want, I can check around. Might be better than you asking questions."

"I don't want any of this getting back to my father."

"Agreed. No good could come out of him knowing. Did you speak with Brent?" Boone mentioned their friend, the local manager at Cattleman's Bank of Western Montana.

"Earlier today. It would be hard for me to qualify for the entire acreage. Somewhere between half and three-quarters of the original land. Anything over half would take up most of my savings, leaving nothing to run the ranch. If all four of us go in, there'd be no issue."

Boone stood, setting his cup in the sink before leaning against the counter, his jaw set. "If the ranch goes up for sale, we're going to be the buyers."

Wicked Waters Saloon rocked along with the music from the live band. Bethany hadn't been inside for weeks, not since meeting her cousin for a drink after work. She'd stayed for less than an hour, while Sarah Mae hadn't left until close to midnight. A typical Friday night for her cousin.

Her gaze swept the packed room, silently hoping Sarah Mae didn't show. Ever since speaking with Larry Lawson about Kell, she carried a sadness which she couldn't dislodge. He hadn't been at the track the last two mornings, another cause for her poor mood. Irritation settled in her chest, knowing Kell not appearing bothered her. She hoped it had nothing to do with their conversation, and her place of employment.

Spotting Sarah Mae at a table in front of the band, Bethany made her way between the tables, avoiding being splashed with beer more than once. Drawing closer, she had the urge to cover her ears, shielding them from the pounding beat. Maybe if she weren't so tired, the music might've appealed more. She glanced up to see Sarah Mae waving at her. To her right sat a handsome young man, his arm draped over the back of her cousin's chair.

"Beth. I knew you'd make it. I ordered you a beer."

A groan escaped before she realized the music would've drowned it out. "Thanks."

"Beth, this is Brock. He works at one of the local ranches."

Standing, he gave a nod in greeting. "Ma'am." Walking around the table, he pulled out her chair.

Prepared to dislike him, Bethany changed her mind. "Thank you, Brock."

Another nod and he retook the chair next to Sarah Mae. This time, his arm settled over her shoulders. The song ended as the waitress set down a round of draft beers.

"How's work going?" Bethany asked the same question each time they met, getting the same answer.

Sarah Mae shrugged. "Same as always." Her cousin worked as an aide at a local nursing home.

"Have you thought more about going back to school?"

Turning toward Brock, Sarah Mae leaned close. "Bethany is always pushing me to get my nursing degree."

"Encouraging you. The decision has always been yours."

"Beth works as a legal assistant and plans to attend law school. It's what she's always wanted to do."

"What do *you* want to do, Sarah Mae?" The question came from Brock, surprising Beth.

"Back in high school, I wanted to be a nurse. After working in the nursing home, I'm not so certain." Sipping her beer, she stared at the stage, then shot a look at Bethany. "Do you think I'd make a good teacher?"

Another surprise. "I think you'll be good at whatever you decide to do. You're great with kids, and you've always loved projects. Remember when you were a counselor at the summer camp? You got great comments."

The table grew silent as the band started a new song. Bethany relaxed, taking small sips of beer while looking around. More people had entered since she arrived, filling all the tables and the bar.

Two men at a table in the back drew her interest. She recognized one as Josh Reyes, a partner with Thorn Macklin and Tony Coletti in Scorpion Custom Motorcycles. The other man sat shadowed in the dark. All she could see was his silhouette. And his eyes. It was his eyes which had her breath catching.

Staring back, Kell lifted his glass, tipping it toward her.

Chapter Five

Beth's heart rate picked up at Kell's acknowledgement. The response frustrated and excited her. After the horrible breakup with the last man she'd dated, Beth believed it would be a long time before her body responded to any man. Apparently, Kell Brooks was the exception.

Giving a slight nod, she shifted away, concentrating on the couples dancing to the country song the band belted out. Sipping her beer, she watched Brock twirl Sarah Mae around the floor, both laughing.

Beth hoped this wasn't one of her fun-loving cousin's male misadventures. She tended to jump head first into new relationships, surprised and hurt when they went nowhere. The thought brought Beth back to the toxic affair she'd ended in Billings. She cringed at the reminder of her stupid decisions.

If it hadn't been for one of her co-workers, she'd have continued seeing the handsome, bright, wealthy, and, she discovered, very married lawyer. The fact she'd believed him when he confirmed on their first date there was no one else in his life, verified the depth of her naiveté.

They'd been seeing each for several months before her friend gently informed Beth of the truth. Not only had he been married, but he had a three-year-old daughter and a baby on the way. Never again would she take a man's word on, well...much of anything.

Lost in her past indiscretion, she didn't notice the music changing to a slow song, startling when a hand settled on her shoulder. Jerking her head up, she stared into amused, ocean blue eyes.

"Sorry to startle you." Kell held out his hand. "Would you care to dance?"

"I, well...I..." Swallowing, she tried to clear her throat.

"It's okay to say no, Bethany Hutchison."

"What? I mean, no. Well, yes." Feeling her face heat, she stood, hoping to recover her usual poise. "I'd like to dance with you."

A wicked smile tipped up the corners of his mouth. "Are you sure?"

Placing her hand in his, she nodded. "Completely."

The song was a ballad, and one of Beth's favorites. She was above average in height, but fit against Kell perfectly. Too much so, she thought, as they began to sway to the music. Getting into the beat, she allowed him to pull her a little closer, her body feeling a slight jolt of recognition. It was as if she belonged right here, in his arms. The reaction caused her to stiffen for an instant before relaxing.

"How long have you been in Whiskey Bend?" His question brought back awareness as to where they were. Two people sharing a dance, nothing more.

"A few months. I left a job in Billings to pursue the opportunity here." She didn't mention her employer, guessing how Kell would react. "I'm taking classes online to finish my bachelor's degree."

"Then on to law school." There was no malice in his voice.

"I hope so. Those classes will have to be at the university."

"So you'll move to Missoula if you're accepted?"

Sighing, she thought of her lack of options. "Probably. Unless I can work something out with Lar...my boss. I heard you work for the Macklins."

He let the error go. Few people knew of his ownership in the ranch. "Yep. I've known them most of my life. Our family ranches shared property lines. They're great people."

"So I've heard. I haven't seen Boone since the night you and I met three years ago."

Kell didn't respond. When the song ended, he kept hold of her hand, escorting her back to the table. "Thank you for the dance, and the company."

Before she could react, he'd turned away, leaving her feeling a bit adrift. An odd sensation, given they didn't know each other well.

"How about another beer?" Sarah Mae looked up at her at the same time Brock pulled out Beth's chair.

"Um, no. It's been a long week. I'm going to head home. Nice to meet you, Brock." Bending down, she kissed her cousin's cheek. "Be safe," she whispered so Brock couldn't hear.

Outside, Beth stared up at a clear, star-filled night. The slight chill in the air had her hustling toward her SUV. Before reaching it, a hand gripped her arm. Whirling around, she grimaced at a face she hoped to never see again.

"Freddy. What are you doing here?" Moving to look around him, she tugged her arm free. "And where's your lovely wife?"

"As if you don't already know."

Taking a step toward her car, she slipped the keys from her purse. "I don't have any idea what you're talking about."

"Thanks to you, she's divorcing me."

Gaze narrowing, she held her ground. "If she found out about your extra marital activities, it wasn't from me. The fact is, I'd hoped no one would ever learn about our time together."

"She found out somehow, and it had to be from you."

"You think I want people to know I dated a complete slimeball like you? It's the opposite. Why don't you go back to Billings and stalk someone else?" Turning, she didn't get two steps away before he gripped her arm in a painful hold, pulling her back.

"Let go of me, Freddy."

"I'd listen to her...Freddy."

Her gaze darting behind him, she let out a relieved breath at the sight of Kell a few feet away. Without hesitating, he stepped around Freddy to rest his arm around Beth's shoulders. Leaning down, he kissed her temple.

"Sorry it took me so long, sweetheart. I had to settle the check." Ignoring Freddy, Kell turned them around, walking down the street toward his truck.

Glancing over her shoulder, she looked at Kell. "My car."

"Yeah. We'll come back for it when your married friend leaves."

Trying to break free, he tugged her against his side, holding her in place. "Calm down, sweetheart. I'm just saving you from your past."

"Saving me?" The words came out on a slight shriek. "I was doing fine without your help."

"Sure you were."

"I know karate."

Chuckling, he steered them toward his truck. "White belt, yellow belt?"

"I'm almost to orange."

"Well, I hope you keep going. To handle a man who's drunk and pissed, you'll need more training." Stopping next to the passenger door, he dropped his arm from her shoulders.

Crossing her arms, she glared at him. "I suppose you're a brown belt."

"Hachidan. Eighth Dan."

Her bravado dropped, as did her arms. "Oh. That's pretty high, right?"

"Yeah. Pretty high. Get in and we'll grab coffee. Give Freddy time to disappear."

She sat stiff as a board while he maneuvered the truck around a few corners, parking at one of the late night coffee bistros new to Whiskey Bend.

Reading the sign, Beth's mouth twisted. "I've never been here."

"Then it will be our first shared experience. Except for Freddy."

Before she could release her seatbelt, Kell had rounded the truck to open her door. Reaching his hand out, he waited when she hesitated.

"Can we just forget all about Frederick Tuttle? He's a mistake I'd hoped to have left behind in Billings."

"Whatever you want." Helping her to the ground, he rested his hand on the small of her back, his gaze moving as they entered the bistro. "Let's get some food, too."

"I'm not real hungry. Coffee would be fine."

"Suit yourself. I'm starving. I hope they have something more than soup and salad, or those awful veggie sandwiches."

Holding in a grin, she stepped up to the counter while perusing the overhead menu. "A medium latte, and..." Checking the board again, and hearing her stomach growl, she looked at the young man. "A spinach and strawberry salad."

"With chicken?"

She pondered an instant. "That would be fine. Thanks." Stepping aside, Beth watched the muscles in Kell's face work as he considered the choices. She doubted any would fulfill his desire for a steak and baked potato.

"The buffalo style burger and fries. Make that a double order of fries. And a coffee. Black." Pulling out his wallet, he laid a twenty on the counter.

The young man's face reddened. "Uh, that's going to be thirty-five dollars, sir."

He set another twenty on top of the first. "Keep the change." Looking beside him, he couldn't miss the laughter on Beth's face. "What?"

"Guess you're used to the prices at Wicked Waters and Doc's Grill."

Shoving the wallet into a back pocket, he took her elbow. "You got that right. Let's get a table."

"I'll pay you back for mine when I get to my car. I left my purse in the SUV."

"No need. Besides, this is the first date I've been on in over three years." Chuckling at the look of shock on Beth's face, he pulled out her chair.

"Three years. You're joking, right?" Sitting down, she clasped her hands together, leaning toward where he sat.

"No, ma'am. Let's just go with the last few years haven't been what I'd imagined. Good, but not how I'd envisioned life."

"You didn't want to work on a ranch?"

"Sure. But the plan was to wait until after I retired from the Army. The fates are still laughing at me."

Beth had so many questions, and no right to ask them. Waiting until their food arrived, she took a bite of salad, chewing while deciding how to satisfy her curiosity.

"What happened to change your plans?"

Swallowing a mouthful of burger, he sipped his coffee. "My last mission didn't go as expected. That wasn't long after we met at the Macklin ranch. The Army gave me a choice of desk duty or medical discharge. I took the discharge and a job at the ranch. End of story." He popped a couple fries in his mouth before picking up the burger for another large bite.

Forking some salad, she now understood why he limped after running the field at the high school. His ending sentence had been so final, Beth didn't dare ask anything more about his last year in the Army. She also knew he wouldn't welcome questions about his family's ranch.

"Do you plan to stay at the Macklins?"

Finishing the burger, he picked up more fries. "I've got a good deal going at the ranch. There's also a chance things will improve more over the next few months." Wiping his mouth with a napkin, he tossed it on the empty plate. "What area of law do you want to practice?" Kell had swiftly turned the tables on her.

"Estate and family law."

"That was quick."

"It's what I've wanted since high school. I may finally get my chance."

Both turned at the sound of the bell above the door chiming. Kell's senses went on immediate alert. Two men walked in dressed in slacks, white shirts, dark ties, and jackets. He knew without asking they were federal of some variety. Without scanning the menu or ordering, the two stopped not a foot away from him.

Kell knew the drill. Both were close to six feet tall, and with him seated, towered over him.

"Staff Sergeant Kellen Brooks?" The older of the two glanced at Beth, then back at him.

"I'm out of the Army, gentlemen. And I'm on a date. Can this wait?"

Without answering, the two pulled out badges, holding them out for Kell to see. "I wondered what alphabet agency you were from. FBI. Impressive. So I ask again, can this wait?"

"Unfortunately, no," the younger of the two answered. "Would you mind coming with us?"

"Look." Kell leaned forward, reading the names. "Agent Sparrow and Agent Rhodes. The lady is riding with me. Let me get her to her car, then we can talk."

"I can walk back, Kell."

"Not a chance, Beth. These good men will wait until I come back. Right, gentlemen?"

Glancing between themselves, Agent Rhodes answered. "We'll follow you."

Knowing he wouldn't get away without hearing what the men had to say, Kell stood, pulling out Beth's chair.

"May I ask what this is about?"

Sparrow lowered his voice. "Do you know a Clifford Walker?"

Body tensing, Kell's jaw hardened. "You already know I do. Why?"

"Someone forced him off the road. He's in critical condition in a Dallas hospital." Retrieving a piece of paper from his pocket, Sparrow held it out to Kell. "He had this in his pocket."

Taking it, Kell closed his eyes a moment before reading the contents.

Kell. They found me.

Chapter Six

Sparrow and Rhodes had commandeered an office in the sheriff's department building. Passing desks occupied by deputies he knew well, Kell gave brief nods to each. Sparrow walked in front of him, Rhodes behind, as if the agents feared he'd bolt. An absurd assumption. He had as many questions for them as they had for him.

Spotting Del in the hall, the agents stopped. Before Rhodes opened his mouth, Del placed fisted hands on his hips, glaring at the men in suits.

"I hope you have a good reason for detaining Kell."

It was then the agents connected the dots. They knew Kell worked as a ranch hand near Whiskey Bend, but hadn't associated the sheriff as one of the owners.

Rhodes recovered quickly. "We just have a few questions for Staff Sergeant Brooks. Shouldn't take long."

"Do you want an attorney present, Kell?"

Eyeing the two agents, he gave a sharp shake of his head. "I'll let you know if I do."

"Fair enough." Del focused on Rhodes. "Let me know if Kell requests one."

Neither agent responded before ushering Kell into a room and closing the door. Rhodes motioned toward a chair. "Have a seat, Staff Sergeant Brooks."

Kell flinched at the use of his former rank. He'd been out of the Army for two years, missed it as he'd miss an arm or leg, and missed the men he called brothers.

"Tell me more about what happened to Cliff."

A smirk appeared on Sparrow's face. "First, we have questions for you."

"Uh-huh. My questions first or I leave."

Sparrow opened his mouth to respond, but Rhodes cut him off. "All right, Sergeant. Ask away. We may or may not have answers for you."

The fast capitulation didn't match with standard FBI behavior. From Kell's experience, which wasn't much, everything hinged on their agenda. They had little sympathy for those they questioned, didn't care if their actions ruined people's lives, and determined guilt in advance. Their job afterward was to prove the guilt. Politics ran rampant, with the biggest goal being the next promotion.

Sparrow fit the description well. The perfect stereotype of a man in pursuit of positive exposure and growing political clout, no matter the cost.

Rhodes was a mystery. Kell guessed him to be in his early fifties, about five-feet-nine, and just a bit overweight. He had the look of a man who enjoyed the gym. Not so much the cardio exercise, which would keep him in top shape. The gold band on his left index finger indicated he was married, or perhaps a widower. At his age, the agent probably had grandchildren.

Leaning forward, Kell rested his muscled arms on the table. "When was the accident?"

Rhodes took a seat across from him. "Yesterday morning about six. His schedule shows he was on his way to his job in downtown Dallas."

"His job being?"

Rhodes lifted a brow. "You don't know?"

"Last I heard, Cliff held a position with a high-level security firm."

Rhodes nodded. "Gemstone Security and Personal Protection, or GSPP. The founders and all operatives are former Army, Marines, Air Force, and Navy with extensive training."

"Special Forces?"

Relaxing, Rhodes noticed Sparrow take a position against a wall and to the right of Kell. "Of one kind or another. He was coming up on two years with the firm. The owners had nothing but praise for his work."

Something in Rhode's tone had Kell narrowing his gaze. "But?"

"Apparently, Walker had some personal issues he refused to discuss. The owners insisted nothing affected his work, but they were concerned. He was driving in a little early to have a meeting with the executives."

"Any idea who ran him off the road?"

Sparrow shoved away from the wall. "That's what we need from you."

"And why would you believe I know?"

Sparrow snorted. "The paper in Walker's pocket. What did he mean by 'they'?"

Rhodes slid the paper across the table toward Kell. "Read it again, Sergeant."

"I know what it says. Doesn't mean I understand it. I haven't seen Cliff in two years, and talked to him no more than three or four times in the last two years."

Rhodes met his gaze. "Does the name Colonel August Hayward mean anything to you?"

Kell's features remained impassive, giving away nothing. "If you're talking about the brigade commander at Fort Lewis, yes."

Rhodes drew Walker's message back toward him, folding it before slipping it into a pocket. "What do you know about him?"

Shrugging, Kell leaned back, letting his hands rest on his thighs. "Not as much as you might think."

Sparrow stepped closer, hovering over Kell. "Come on, Brooks. He's the commanding officer of the 75th Ranger Regiment at Fort Lewis. Hayward held the same position when you were a squad commander."

"Doesn't mean I knew much about him. We were one of many special operations units under his command. We executed orders."

"But you met him." A knowing grin flickered across Sparrow's chiseled face.

"Sure, I did. As did a lot of others in the 2nd Ranger Battalion. That's about six hundred men." Kell shifted toward Rhodes. "Is there a point to this?"

"Of the eight squad members on your last operation, four men returned alive. All left the Rangers within a year.

Of those, Specialist Robert Moser died in a crash similar to the one that put Specialist Walker in the hospital. Do you believe in coincidences, Sergeant?"

Kell didn't respond.

"You and Corporal Zane Talbot are the only two left out of a squad of eight. What does that tell you?"

"Honestly, Agent Rhodes, not much. Four men died during extraction from the operation three years ago. Those are combat deaths, and have nothing to do with what happened to Moser and Walker."

Crossing one leg over the other, Rhodes relaxed, clasping his hands in his lap. Waiting a few beats, he pinned Kell with an even stare. "Are you certain of that?"

Right now, he wasn't certain of anything. There were things he knew, the same as all eight men on his squad had known.

Assuming Walker lived, there were now three men left. Could the four deaths during their extraction be anything other than an attack by enemy combatants? Was it possible the deaths had been orchestrated? Were four men murdered three years ago, leaving four more as targets? Kell didn't like the way this was playing out, or the deep rage beginning to build inside him.

He needed to get out of there so he could contact Talbot to discuss what his squad had learned before their last mission. The information was damning, the stuff that ruined careers, and sent men to prison. Was there a chance any of this was tied together? Could what was going on have anything to do with the shot fired at Kell?

Checking the time, he stood. "Well, gentlemen, this has been quite educational. Unfortunately, I have somewhere to be. Maybe we can do this again sometime."

"Sit down, Brooks." Sparrow's face had gone from smug to furious in a few heartbeats.

"Sergeant Brooks is right, Sparrow. We know where he works. Besides, he's a close friend of the sheriff." Joining Kell at the door, Rhodes handed him a card before resting his hand on the knob. "Until next time, Sergeant."

Beth hadn't been able to sleep for more than an hour at a time, then laid awake another hour before dozing off. Her mind wouldn't let go of the happenings at the bistro.

She'd never had firsthand experience with any federal agents. Nothing up close and personal as it had been earlier that night. The conversation played over and over in her head, ruining the sleep Beth craved.

Watching as the FBI agents pulled out behind Kell, she'd felt the strongest urge to follow, make certain they treated him right. Silly, yet consistent with her strong sense of right and wrong, the deep concern for those she cared about. Somehow, over a remarkably short time, Kell fell into the group of people she wanted to protect.

Closing her eyes, she grimaced at another ridiculous thought. Of all the people she knew, Kell Brooks needed protection the same as she needed another relationship. Not at all.

The weekend passed in boring monotony. She ran, finished errands, then tackled her studies. There'd been no word from Kell, yet she hadn't expected anything. By Sunday night, she'd put the entire event behind her. At least, that had been the plan.

When her alarm chimed at six-thirty Monday morning, she dragged herself from the bed, wondering what had happened with Kell and the agents, and if he was all right. Three times she'd dialed the number at the ranch, hanging up before anyone answered.

They weren't a couple. Were barely friends. She had no right to follow-up, even if it was out of concern. A relationship with anyone held no appeal. Except maybe...

"Beth, line four is for you."

"Who is it, Alana?"

"Kellen Brooks. Should I take a message?"

She knew she should say *yes*. It would be the smart thing to do. "No, I'll take it." Letting out a slow breath, she picked up the phone. "Hello, Kell."

"Beth. Did I catch you at a bad time?"

"This is fine. I'll be leaving in half an hour. What can I do for you?"

"Nothing, really. Just wanted to make sure you were all right."

"You mean after the FBI swept you away to parts unknown?"

Despite the odd activity of a couple nights before, his chuckle had her grinning. "We went to the sheriff's office. Del was there."

"They didn't lead you away in handcuffs?"

"Nothing that dramatic. A few questions and I left. Look, I need to go, but wanted to make sure you're okay."

Beth felt a swell of warmth at his concern. "I'm fine, Kell. By the way, I still owe you for dinner."

"Let's call it even. Take care of yourself. I'll see you around." With that, he ended the call, leaving her feeling unsettled, and a little empty.

She didn't know what she'd expected. It hadn't been a real date. The truth was, he'd saved her from what could've turned into an embarrassing confrontation with Freddy. Staring at the phone, she sighed.

"Yeah. See you around, Kell."

Chapter Seven

Kell thought of the call, believing he'd made a mistake not asking to see Beth again. They'd had a good time. Right up until Agents Rhodes and Sparrow had interrupted them. The timing couldn't be more wrong for him to start anything, especially with a woman who worked for a law firm he had every intention of never working with again. Still, Kell couldn't shake the feeling he'd be missing out on something important.

Holding the phone in his hand, he made a quick decision. "This is Kellen Brooks again. Is Bethany Hutchison available?"

He could hear the slight amusement in the woman's voice. "Let me check for you, Mr. Brooks." A moment later, Beth took the call.

"Forget something, Kell?"

"Any chance you're free for dinner tonight at Wicked Waters or Doc's Grill?" Closing his eyes, he wondered what the hell he was doing. He didn't need entanglements, especially now.

"Meet you at Doc's at seven?"

Straightening in his chair, he juggled the phone, almost dropping it on the floor. "Great. Perfect. See you at seven."

Ending the call, Kell felt an unaccustomed sense of anticipation. Two hours until he'd meet Beth. Plenty of time to think about the craziness in his life.

Agent Rhodes had remained silent over the weekend, giving Kell time to piece together his next steps. Or maybe the agent had lost interest, found another thread to follow.

"Not a chance," Kell told himself.

He'd spent most of the day riding the fence lines on the western edge of the property. Close to where he'd been when someone fired on him. A threat to his life or a warning? He had no idea. After the encounter with Sparrow and Rhodes, Kell planned to pass along what happened to the agents. Might not mean much to the men, or be worth their time investigating.

With most of his team dead, Walker fighting for his life, and him and Talbot still in danger, Kell had no desire to be a hero. He'd placed himself in the tentacles of danger many times as an Army Ranger. He now rode for the Macklin brand, and was proud to be a part of it.

The lack of response from Zane Talbot over the weekend concerned him. Five messages without a reply. By late Sunday, he'd called Zane's parents to see if he might be at their ranch. They hadn't picked up. Not wanting to worry them, Kell didn't leave a message.

The same reason he hadn't discussed the FBI's visit with Boone and Thorn. All Del knew was what he saw at the station, which amounted to nothing. They had enough going on without being brought into whatever the FBI had in mind.

When the wall clock chimed six o'clock, Kell punched in Zane's number again. It rang five times before Zane's voicemail picked up.

"It's Kell. Call me. We have to talk."

He'd already checked Cliff's progress at the Dallas hospital, learning his friend was stable with mild improvement. They'd suggested he call again tomorrow and talk to the doctor.

Changing clothes, Kell began to doubt his decision to meet Beth for dinner. Reminding himself it was just a meal didn't stop the uncertainty lodging in his chest. It had been too long since he'd spent time with a woman. Other than the Macklin wives, there'd been no meetups for coffee or a meal.

The drive took less than twenty minutes. Parking a block away, he stood on the sidewalk, swiping damp palms down his jeans. Not wanting Beth to stand alone waiting, he closed the distance to Doc's.

He reached the front door at the same time Beth walked up. "Hey."

"Hi, Kell."

Opening the door, he motioned for her to enter first, both stopping to inhale the wonderful aroma coming from the kitchen. Before a minute passed, Doc came walking toward them, a huge smile on his face.

"Kell, my man. It's been a long time." Their bro-hug brought a grin to Beth's face.

"I was in here a couple weeks ago."

"Still too long." Doc took in the woman next to Kell. "And who is this lovely lady?"

She held out her hand. "Beth Hutchison. I've been in here a few times since moving to Whiskey Bend. The food is wonderful."

Taking her hand between both of his, he looked at Kell. "She's a beauty. Perhaps you should keep her."

"Keep her?" Beth squeaked out. "Maybe I don't want to keep him." Her joking tone confirmed she was teasing.

"See, Kell. A woman with a mind of her own. Where would you like to sit?"

Choosing a table by the window, both ordered drinks while checking the menu. "I don't know why I bother looking. I always get one of two items." Kell closed the menu, setting it aside.

"Let me guess. The meat lasagna or spaghetti with meatballs."

Tossing up his hands, Kell chuckled. "You got me."

"So, which will it be tonight?"

Kell looked at Beth. "What are you having?"

"Does it matter?"

"It does if I want to share."

It was Beth's turn to laugh. "You plan on eating off my plate?"

He grinned, all innocence. "Isn't that what sharing's about?"

Shaking her head, she looked at Doc. "The chicken martini."

"Great choice. Would you prefer lasagna or spaghetti, Kell?"

Beth handed her menu back to Doc. "You're serious about sharing."

Kell's features sobered. "I'm always serious about food."

"Good to know." Picking up her wine glass, she tipped it toward him. "What shall we toast to?"

Kell didn't hesitate. "Dinner with a beautiful woman."

Feeling her face flush, she touched the edge of his glass. "And an intriguing man."

"Would you care for more coffee?" The young waitress held up a carafe of coffee.

"A little more for me." Kell wasn't ready to end what had been a wonderful evening.

"The same."

The waitress filled Kell's cup, then Beth's before picking up their empty dessert plates and leaving them alone. Their conversation until then had centered on her classes and his work at the ranch. Neither had touched on subjects which might be difficult, such as Kell's family ranch, her employment with Lawson and Chapman, or what happened Friday after he left with the FBI.

Though she didn't want to pry, Beth wanted to learn more about him, a man with many layers. She hadn't lied when admitting she found him intriguing.

"How do you like working with Larry Lawson?"

The question surprised her. He'd made it clear he didn't care for the man or his law firm. Beth found herself weighing how to respond. Honesty always worked best for her.

"Larry is a wonderful boss, as is Janet Chapman. I was fortunate to land a position with them."

"I'm sure the position garnered a lot of interest." Taking a sip of coffee, Kell lowered the cup.

"Larry said they had close to a hundred applicants. Many from out of the area, and some from out of state. The firm has an excellent reputation."

"Most people I know use them."

Adding a little more cream to her coffee, she took a sip, not sure what Kell wanted to know. "I hope to stay with them as long as possible."

"Larry knows your plans?"

"Yes. I was quite open with him and Janet when interviewing for the job. They already knew the law school requires all onsite classes. Both were open to having me work part-time. Much will depend on when classes are offered. Who knows, I might return to waitressing. That is, if I get accepted."

"There's no doubt in my mind you'll get accepted, Beth. I heard Larry is an adjunct law professor at Missoula. I'm sure his recommendation will help."

"I hope so. If not, I'll have to consider applying out of state, which isn't what I want." Taking another sip from her cup, she set it down. "What are your plans, Kell? Do you plan to stay at the Macklin ranch?"

"I'm not going anywhere, Beth. The Macklins have been good to me. When my father sold the family ranch without so much as a letter, the brothers offered me a fifteen percent interest in their ranch. The four of us have plans to expand. From where I'm sitting, the future looks pretty darn good."

A wistful smile tipped up the corners of her mouth. "You sound so confident in your future. I envy you, Kell."

A frown twisted his features. "No one should envy me, Beth. Certainly not you."

Finishing her coffee, she rested both elbows on the table, threading her fingers together. "What exactly did you do in the Army?"

Leaning back in the chair, he stretched out his long legs while studying her face. Hers was a sincere question, one he'd answered several times in the same way.

"The same as anyone else. Whatever my commander ordered my squad to do."

"Which eventually forced you out of the Army."

"Some things are out of anyone's control, Beth. Most missions go well. Others don't. It's the way of the world."

Though after the conversation with Rhodes and Sparrow, a thread of doubt had grown in Kell's chest. What if his squad's extraction had been meant to fail?

Walking Beth to her car, he couldn't stop himself from scanning the area in search of danger. Old habits die hard. Even more so for a former Army Ranger. Stopping next to her SUV, he took another look around, seeing nothing to worry him.

"Thank you for dinner, Kell. I had a wonderful time."

"I'm glad you had time to join me." Bending down, he brushed a kiss across her cheek. "Perhaps we can do it again."

"I'd like that. Have a good night." With a last look at Kell, she slipped inside.

"You do the same, Beth."

Kell's thoughts moved between Beth, Cliff, and Zane as he worked the following day. He knew his friends, and former squad members, had to take priority right now. One held onto life by a thread. And the other? Kell didn't know what was going on with Zane or if he was in danger.

What he did know was Beth didn't belong in his life right now. Maybe never. But he was becoming a weak man where she was concerned. Kell craved her company, wanted to learn everything he could about the spirited Ms. Hutchison.

Getting his strength back and working the ranch had been all he could handle over the last three years. There'd been little time to think about women, and a future which might include a family.

Living with Boone, Willow, and Tyler, he couldn't help but feel a little envious. That life was still a long way beyond his means. The Macklin brothers were settled, at a stage in their lives where a family made sense. Not so with Kell.

Beth Hutchison made him long for what was too far out of his reach. She deserved a man better than him. One who hadn't done the things required of Kell during his time in the Rangers. Someone without the demons and nightmares, which still marred his life.

As true as those thoughts were, Kell knew he wasn't ready to give her up. Wouldn't forgo the pleasure of her company. At least not for a little while longer.

Chapter Eight

Amy and Del had arrived that evening, bringing with them a large pot filled with the best stew Kell had eaten in a long time. Willow was a great cook, but Amy had the lock on stew and pies, while Thorn's wife, Grace, fixed incredible Mexican fare.

The three couples, plus Kell and Tyler, didn't leave even a small amount of leftovers. An hour later, with Tyler tucked into bed, the seven adults discussed what was needed to buy part or all of the original Brooks' ranch.

Almost out of operating cash, the Jernigans had decided to put the entire spread up for sale. According to what they'd told Willow while at the feed store, Jim had received an excellent employment offer near Austin, Texas. One they couldn't turn down.

She'd called Boone within minutes of the couple leaving the store. He, Thorn, Del, and Kell had met with the bank manager later that afternoon, determined not to let the ranch slip through their hands.

Thorn studied the map Boone spread out on the kitchen table. "Buying all two thousand acres will give us a total of thirty-six hundred. Plenty to do whatever we want."

Del tapped a spot on the map, then two others. "There are places where it would be easy to add roads if we wanted to subdivide the acreage."

Boone's brows furrowed. "Subdivide?"

"You know. Like what goes on in several other states. Thirty-five to forty acre parcels."

Thorn nodded. "Not a bad idea, Del. We don't need all thirty-six hundred acres. Not unless we plan to run more cattle." He glanced around the table. "Anyone thinking in that direction?"

Boone rubbed his stubbled chin, feeling Willow's hand on his thigh. It was a reminder on their discussion about the new technologies and methods to raise cattle on smaller amounts of land.

"If we do decide to increase the herd, we still wouldn't need all the land. Half would be plenty."

Kell nodded his agreement. "Leaving us eighteen hundred acres available to subdivide or sell off in larger chunks. We just want to be careful how we do it."

"We also talked about carving out parcels for each of us to build a house. Five or ten acres is all Grace and I want." Thorn looked at his wife, who offered a slow grin.

"Same with me and Amy. Kell? What are you thinking?"

"Haven't thought too much about it. Knowing the horse side of our business is where I'm comfortable, I'd be looking at thirty to fifty acres."

Boone shoved his chair back and stood. Grabbing the coffeepot, he filled his cup before offering it to others. Leaning his hip against the counter, he blew across the hot liquid before taking a sip.

"I want no less than three hundred acres deeded in my name."

"I don't have a problem with that," Thorn said. "And I don't have an issue with Kell having more acreage deeded to him. You two are the ones here every day, and I don't see that changing for a long time."

Their meeting had broken up not long after Thorn's pronouncement. Kell sat at the desk in his bedroom, staring at a mobile phone, which offered no answers to his growing questions.

He'd tried calling Zane again, leaving another message. Not ready to sleep, his next call was to the hospital in Dallas.

"My name's Kellen Brooks. I'm a good friend, and former squad commander, of Clifford Walker. Is there any news on his progress?"

"Are you family?"

A frustrated breath burst from him. "No. But we're as close as brothers."

After a long silence, the nurse asked him to hang on while she checked with the doctor on call. Several minutes later, the doctor came on the line.

"Mr. Brooks?"

"Yes."

"I'm Doctor Teresa Lang. Since you're Mr. Walker's emergency contact, I'll give you what I can. He's still in critical condition. The good news is he's improving a little every day."

Relief flooded through him. "That is good news. Any idea when he might be able to talk to me?"

"Not at this time. I...just a minute. I'm sorry, Mr. Brooks, but I have to go. I'll call you if there's any change."

"Wait." But she'd already ended the call.

An hour later, the phone rang. He recognized the hospital's prefix. "Brooks."

"Mr. Brooks, it's Doctor Lang." She sounded tired, and something else.

"Yes?"

"I'm sorry to inform you Mr. Walker has had a setback. He experienced a heart attack. We worked on him for quite a while before getting a response. He slipped into a coma not long afterward. I'm very sorry there isn't better news."

Forcing calm, his mind raced with what to ask. "Had you uncovered any heart problems?"

"None. His heart was strong. We'll be doing extensive testing, and either I or someone else will keep you informed."

"Thank you, Doctor Lang. I appreciate you calling me back."

"Of course. Feel free to check back if you don't hear from anyone."

Ending the call, he dropped his phone onto the desk, face in his hands. As the doctor confirmed, Cliff's heart had been fine, strong and healthy. Why a heart attack while he'd been improving from the car wreck?

Grabbing the phone, he called Zane once more. This time, his friend picked up. Kell couldn't keep the intense irritation from his voice.

"Where have you been? I've left several messages."

"Calm down, buddy. I've been working nonstop for three days to complete a project. What's up?"

"Cliff had a heart attack tonight."

"What happened?"

"That's why I've been trying to reach you. The same as Brian, Cliff was run off the road. He's been in the hospital a few days. According to the doctor I spoke with earlier tonight, Cliff was improving. I was on the phone with her when he went into cardiac arrest. He's now in a coma."

"I can't believe this. Cliff's heart was strong. Something isn't right, Kell."

"Agreed. Where will you be tomorrow?"

"Wherever you need me to be. I've been thinking about what you said. I'd like to speak with Del."

"Glad to hear it. Call me with flight details and I'll pick you up. In the meantime, watch your back. With Cliff in a coma, it's down to you and me, Zane."

"We'll talk as soon as I get there. You know what I mean. Right, Kell?"

The cold beer felt good rolling down his throat. Kell sat on the top rail of the corral with Zane Friday afternoon, watching as two foals danced around the open space. It had been two long days, numerous calls to Dallas, and several talks with Zane, but they'd reached an agreement.

They weren't Rangers anymore. Their skills weren't sharp, and the thrill of the hunt had ceased long ago. Still, they had to do something about what they'd learned while still in the Army, while protecting themselves from what happened to Brian and Cliff.

Kell lifted his bottle, pointing it toward Zane. "I'm meeting Thorn and his friends at Wicked Waters tonight. You're coming with me."

"I'm pretty beat, Kell. Doubt I'd be much fun."

"We'll have a beer at Wicked Waters, then head over to Doc's. It'll do you good."

Zane had flown into Missoula fifteen hours after talking with Kell. He'd been granted a one month leave of absence. Zane doubted he'd return. The money had been good, the work interesting, his fellow employees smart, but with little life experience.

It hadn't been as easy as expected to move from being a skilled Army Ranger to consulting for a gaming company. Being outside, working with horses, felt good. He still had twenty-eight days to make a decision.

Zane slid to the ground. "Fine. I've got a few more chores to complete before cleaning up. What time are you planning to leave?"

"Be ready at six." Kell joined him, heading to the barn while Zane met Cody on the other side of the house, where they worked together, making repairs to the stackyard.

Tomorrow, they'd take the flatbed trailer down the road to pick up the bales used around the nearby pastures and barn. One large load would fill the stackyard for several weeks.

Saddling Joker, Kell decided to ride out to the western edge and make a large turn along the backside of what had been his family's ranch. The Macklins and Kell would be meeting with Brent Nance at the bank on Monday to make on offer on the two thousand acres. The thought had Kell's stomach twisted in knots.

Del knew the property hadn't been listed with a local realtor, and an internet search brought up nothing. If luck was with them, they might close the deal before anyone else knew about the sale.

Riding across the last pasture, Kell glanced toward the spot where the bullet had barely missed him. As with each time he thought about that day, anger grew in his chest. In the old days, he'd have had his gun out and been moving toward the shooter's location within seconds of the shot. A respected staff sergeant in the elite Army Rangers had flattened himself on the ground, his mind going blank.

Biting back a curse at how he'd handled the incident, Kell continued along his route, checking the fence line as he rode. Sliding to the ground, he unlocked a little used gate at the far northwestern corner of the Macklin ranch. It connected their spread with the original Brooks property.

Kell and Boone had used it often while growing up. Sneaking out to go fishing. Visiting each other when one's parents were out for the night.

So many good times flashed through Kell's mind as he walked his horse through the opening, and relocked the gate. Too many memories to count. One adventure after another, each one developing them into men people could trust. At the time, they had no idea how each discovery formed a small building block, education they'd draw upon throughout their lives.

An odd out of body experience flowed over him as he rode the fence line where he grew up. Several yards ahead, he spotted the giant sycamore he climbed as a boy. The same tree he tumbled from, breaking a wrist and twisting an ankle.

Kell knew if he rode around it, he'd see the initials carved into the tree as a sophomore in high school. KB and JA. Kellen Brooks and June Allerby. He'd been in love for the first time. Three weeks later, June decided another boy was more interesting and broke off their short-lived relationship. He'd been heartbroken. Today, the memory brought only amusement.

Beyond the tree stood the storage shed he'd helped his father construct between his junior and senior year of high school. It didn't appear to have been touched in all the years since.

Stopping outside of it, he dismounted, ground tying Joker. Walking around the outside, Kell grimaced at the lack of repair, the weathered wood, some planks he was certain were rotten.

One dirt encrusted window had been installed to let light inside. Walking back to the front, he looked around. He knew the Jernigans didn't have any hired help, and the odds Jim or Connie would be out this way was minimal.

Touching the knob, he looked around one more time before turning it, surprised when the door opened. As if it had been oiled recently. Surprised, he pushed. The hinges didn't squeak, nor did the aged wood scrape against the threshold or plank floor.

An odd sense of foreboding wrapped around him as he took a step inside. Glancing around, he saw nothing to cause alarm. Then he shoved the door all the way open and stilled.

Against one wall was an open crate. Taking a step closer, anger gripped him. Bricks of some kind of white substance were packed in plastic wrap.

Whispering a curse, he walked closer, confirming what was inside the crate. He guessed them to be bricks of cocaine. Letting out a breath, he whirled back toward the door at a muffled whimper.

Lowering himself into a crouch, he reached behind him to the holster at his back, withdrawing his Ruger Blackhawk .44 mag. A sense of calm claimed him as he assessed the situation.

Again, the sound came. A whimper consistent with a wounded animal. And it came from behind him.

Twisting, the gun out in front of him, he sucked in a stunned breath. Against the wall with the dirt encrusted window sat a woman. Wrists and ankles bound, tape over her mouth, her huge, round eyes locked with his.

Eyes pleading for help.

Chapter Nine

Years of training kicked into action. Dragging his phone from a pocket, Kell took a series of pictures. Of the woman, the crate, the inside of the shed. Then he called Boone, explaining what he'd found.

Placing a finger over his lips, Kell knelt in front of the woman, removing the handkerchief used to silence her before using his knife to cut the ties which bound her. Wide, panicked eyes locked on his as her fingers dug into his arms.

"They'll be back. We have to leave." He couldn't miss the fear in her shrill voice. "Please. Before they come back for me."

"A friend will be here any minute to take you to the hospital."

She shook her head violently. "No hospital. Just get me away from here."

"I'm Kell. What's your name?"

Swallowing, her gaze kept moving about the small space. "Trudy. My name is Trudy."

"All right, Trudy. This is what's going to happen. I'm on horseback, so my friend, Boone, will take you back to the ranch. We'll check your injuries before calling the sheriff."

"No. They'll kill me."

"No one's going to hurt you. I'll protect you, as will my friends. One of them is the sheriff. He'll know what to do."

The sound of a siren in the distance caught his attention, as did Boone's voice. "Kell. You in there?"

"Come on in."

Taking a step inside, Boone saw the crate and whistled. "What is it?"

"Cocaine. I think. This is Trudy. Trudy, this is Boone Macklin. She was bound and gagged when I found her. Did you call Del?"

"Yeah. It's best if he sees this for himself." Boone's focus didn't waver from Trudy. "Hold on."

Dashing outside, he returned seconds later with a bottle of water. The men watched as she took several gulps, stopping her before she became sick.

The siren grew louder, then faded. Boone poked his head outside and waved. "Del's here. Joe Nolen's with him." He mentioned one of Del's deputies.

Attempting to stand, Trudy's knees almost gave out before Kell took her arm. "Give yourself a minute. How long were you tied up?"

She stared at the floor. "I don't know. Sometime yesterday."

Kell shot Boone a look, knowing his friend felt the same rising anger as him.

"Let's get you outside, Trudy. Sheriff Macklin is waiting." Kell put a hand at her elbow, guiding her toward the door.

She stopped, her body shaking. "They'll see me. I was told to stay inside."

"That's before these boys found you." Del closed the distance between them. "I'm Sheriff Macklin. What's your name, ma'am?"

"Trudy."

"What's your last name, Trudy?"

Letting out a trembling breath, she didn't look at any of the men. "Loomis." She said it as if scared they might recognize it.

Del glanced at the others. George Loomis, a member of the Blackfoot tribe, lived off the reservation in a stately home with a view of the Bitterroot Mountains. Well respected, he had to be in his seventies. "Are you related to George?"

Her hesitancy told Del what he wanted, but he still needed to hear it from her. "Trudy?"

"Yes. He's my grandfather."

"Excellent. I'll call him."

She leaped at Del, hitting the hand holding his phone. It landed a few feet away. The uncontrolled panic caused her breath to catch, and she bent over, trying to suck in air.

Kell placed a broad hand on her back, rubbing up and down. "Calm down, Ms. Loomis. Take slow breaths."

Trudy did as he said, working to get her breathing even.

"You can't tell my grandfather." She choked out the statement, still fighting to breathe. "No one can know what happened."

Del knelt in front of her, lowering his voice. "All right, for now. We'll go the clinic, then to my office, where you can give me your statement. Afterward, we'll discuss what to do next."

Standing, he looked into the shed. "Joe. Were you able to get a hold of your contact at the DEA?"

"Sure thing, boss. He'll get to Whiskey Bend as soon as he can. Do you want me to hang around here, or should we haul the product to the office?"

Del didn't like the idea of leaving Joe alone with a haul worth hundreds of thousands of dollars. "Take photos, then we'll load the crate into Boone's truck. You okay following me to the office, Boone?"

"No problem. I'll bring Kell with me." Boone turned toward him. "Ride Joker back to the ranch. I'll pick you up on my way."

"Joe and I will follow you to the ranch, then we'll head to the sheriff's station. In case the owners of the crate are watching, I don't want anyone to be a lone target."

Kell mounted Joker, taking a shortcut to the Macklin ranch. He arrived a little before Boone and Del. Trudy sat in the back seat of Del's SUV, head down, body shaking. The blanket Joe gave her had done little to still her trembling.

Del waited on the main road for Kell to jump into Boone's truck for the trip to the clinic. All men were armed. All vigilant, aware of the danger hovering over them.

Kell kept watch to the sides and behind them, knowing Joe did the same in the SUV. He'd known the Sinaloa Cartel had a foothold in Washington and Oregon. The news showed an increase in arrests in Idaho and Montana. He couldn't recall if those arrests were cartel related or not.

Parking at the clinic, Kell jumped out, taking what he hoped to be a casual stance at the corner of the truck. The crate had been covered with a tarp held down with rope. Unless they'd been followed, no one would associate the large, bulky item with what had been discovered in the shed.

They'd been at the clinic less than five minutes when two more sheriff department SUVs pulled into the lot, surrounding the truck. When Del and Joe appeared with Trudy, the four vehicles drove straight to the sheriff station.

Two DEA agents and a federal van awaited them. Once the crate was transferred, the bricks inventoried, and their statements taken, Boone and Kell were cleared to leave.

"I don't feel right taking off without saying something to Trudy."

Boone clasped Kell on the shoulder. "She's locked down. They're not going to let you see her. You saved Trudy from whatever hell her captors had planned. Let it go, Kell. You've done all you can."

He'd left, but now, a few hours later, guilt at not checking on Trudy still bothered him. Touching the glass to his lips, Kell took a slow draw of ice cold beer.

Kull Kacey, the owner of Wicked Waters, sat on one side of him, Zane on the other. Thorn Macklin and his business partners, Josh Reyes and Tony Coletti, took up the remaining chairs.

Few seats remained in Kull's popular saloon. He brought the best bands in on Fridays and Saturdays, and it often seemed every local came out to hear them.

Surrounded by friends, Kell couldn't shake an odd sense of isolation. Nor could he pinpoint the cause. The music didn't appeal to him, the beer tasted flat, and the large crowd pressed in on him. Kell knew those were excuses for what weighed on him.

It had been days since he'd spoken with Beth. Zane's arrival, and the discovery of Trudy Loomis, had allowed little time for anything personal. Again, an excuse for not calling her.

He hoped to find her in Wicked Waters with her cousin. Sarah sat at a table up front with the same cowboy as a week earlier. Beth wasn't with them.

A gentle nudge to his shoulder had him shifting to look at Zane. "Yeah?"

"You ready to get out of here and get some food?"

Finishing the remaining beer, Kell stood. "We're out of here, guys. We'll be at Doc's if anyone wants to join us." No one moved, indicating the others had dug in for the night.

Walking the short distance to the restaurant, they found it as busy as Wicked Waters. Kell gave a chin lift or smile to several people he knew, introduced Zane, and made small talk until a table near the kitchen opened up.

It wasn't long before Doc spotted them. "Kell. It's good to see you."

Accepting Doc's outstretched hand, he nodded next to him. "Doc, this is Zane Talbot. We served together. He moved here a few days ago to work with me at the ranch."

"Welcome to Whiskey Bend, Zane." The two shook hands before Doc offered menus. "Take a look while I get you samples of a new appetizer." He shoved the door to the kitchen open, disappearing into what was considered the heart of the restaurant.

"Doc's always trying out new dishes."

"Are they any good?" Zane sipped his water while glancing around the moderate-sized business.

"They're all excellent. He doesn't offer anything not a hundred percent to his liking. The thing is, none ever appear on the menu. It's a real shame."

"Here you are." Doc set a small plate with four raviolis on the table.

Zane held back scooping one onto his fork as he wanted. "What's in them?"

"Try one and I'll tell you."

The four raviolis vanished in less than a minute. "These are great, Doc."

"Thanks, Kell. They're a variation of my aunt's recipe. Ricotta, spinach, and pesto with a garlic, white wine sauce. There's more to the recipe, but I can't divulge all my secrets. What will you boys have tonight?"

"Sausage lasagna for me, with house salad, and a glass of the new craft beer."

Doc didn't write anything down before looking at Zane. "For you?"

"The same."

Crystal clear, female laughter came from the doorway, drawing all three men's attention.

"Friday night and two beautiful women are alone. You boys ought to consider rectifying that. I'll seat them and get your orders started."

A lump formed in Kell's throat at the sight of Beth. She looked stunning in black capri length slacks, three-inch black heels, and a deep peach colored top, which hugged her breasts. Her appearance drew the attention of several men who openly stared, including Zane.

"I'm targeting the taller one."

"She's taken, Zane."

Brow lifting, a grin appeared on his face. "Yeah?"

"We're dating. Sort of."

Doc steered the women toward an empty table near Kell and Zane. He saw the instant her gaze landed on him. Stopping, she dropped her purse onto the seat, making no move toward him.

Standing, he closed the distance between them. "Hello, Beth."

"Kell. How are you?"

"It's been a helluva week. This is Zane Talbot. We were in the Army together."

Rising, Zane held out his hand. "It's a pleasure, ma'am."

"Nice to meet you, Zane. This is my friend, Alana. We work together. Kell, I believe you two have met."

"Mr. Brooks. It's good to see you again."

He gave a curt nod, remembering the scene he'd made in Larry Lawson's office. Alana had rushed in at his raised voice. It wasn't his best hour.

Noting the tension between the two, Zane motioned toward the table. "Why don't you ladies join us?"

Beth opened her mouth to decline when Kell took her hand. "We'd enjoy the company." He wanted to confess how much he'd missed her, choosing to let the thought go for now.

"If you're sure?"

"Absolutely." Zane answered for both of them as he pulled out a chair for Alana.

Kell did the same for Beth, letting his hand linger longer than normal on her shoulder before moving to his own chair.

They chatted through dinner, Zane telling them about the job he left in California, and Kell describing the births of two more foals during the last week. No one mentioned their time in the Army.

Tilting up the bottle, Kell took another swallow of his beer. "Anything new at work you can talk about, Beth?"

"Not really."

Alana's brows drew together. "That's not quite accurate. We have a real interesting new case Larry and Janet will be working on together."

"What case is that?" Zane asked.

Ignoring Beth's warning look, Alana lowered her voice. "It's been in the local paper and on the radio, so you've probably read about it. We're representing a local property owner who's considered a person of interest."

"Over what?" Kell winced, thinking he already knew.

Beth answered for Alana. "His possible involvement in the detainment of a woman found on his property."

Chapter Ten

Zane's eyes grew wide. "Detainment. As in kidnapping? That would be a felony, right?"

Kell shot a warning look at his friend. So far, the identities of Kell and Boone hadn't been mentioned in any stories regarding the woman's discovery. From their expressions, he didn't believe Beth or Alana knew they were involved.

Beth glanced at Zane. "If he's arrested. The sheriff is still investigating. We don't know if any charges will be filed. We don't believe the sheriff has found any evidence our client knew the woman was being held on his property."

"The woman's grandfather is understandably angry. He's looking for justice," Alana added.

Zane massaged the back of his neck while moving it from side to side, stretching the tight muscles. "I'd assume he wants the actual kidnappers arrested."

Beth's mouth drew into a taut line. "If they can be identified."

Lifting her gaze to Kell, she bit her lower lip, knowing this could hold up the sale of the ranch he so desperately wanted back. She could tell by the look in his eyes he knew it, too.

"We know the grandfather has contacted another firm in town to represent his granddaughter."

Kell's brow rose. "For what?"

"We don't know. Larry Lawson is his personal attorney. Since the property owner contacted Larry first, the firm committed to represent him if charges are filed. We couldn't represent both."

Leaning forward, Kell rested one arm on the table. "Who'd he hire?"

Beth did something Kell hadn't expected. She smirked. "Mick Vogel."

"You don't like Vogel?" Kell asked.

Alana couldn't hold back a snort. "He's been trying to get to know Beth better since she came to town."

Features impassive, Kell speared Beth with a look. "You dated him?"

"Not really. We met for lunch once. What he wants is for me to leave Lawson and Chapman to work for him. It will never happen."

Chuckling to mask the relief coursing through him, an idea began to form. "How about you two ladies come out to the ranch tomorrow to see the new foals?"

"I'd love to." Alana's instant response had the men smiling.

"I can't. I'm buried in homework."

Alana stared at her. "You rarely study on Saturdays, Beth. Let's go out for a quick look at the foals, then I'll get you home. You'll have the entire afternoon and Sunday to immerse yourself in books."

Reaching out, Kell entwined his fingers with Beth's, a gesture not missed by Zane and Alana. "Come on out. It's been a long time since you've seen the ranch."

Alana glanced at Zane, lifting a brow. "That makes two of us, Beth. Few people get to see foals at this young age."

A slow smile spread across Beth's face. "All right."

"I'll drive," Alana offered before Beth could change her mind. "It's going to be amazing."

Alana was right. Beth couldn't take her eyes off the foals. Two colts and two fillies had been born over the last two weeks. Although she'd grown up on her family's ranch outside of Billings, the sight of foals never failed to touch her. Eyes filled with excitement met Kell's.

"They're beautiful. Will you be keeping or selling them?"

"All four are for specific clients. Most foals have been sold prior to birth. We keep a few every year. The agreements are we keep the colts and fillies for two years minimum."

"So the owners have no access to them?"

Kell rested his arms on the top rail of the corral. "They have full access, but they must notify us in advance they'll be coming by. Most give us a day, although some call thirty minutes in advance. We just want to know they'll be here. The owners can also remove animals from here prior to two years with appropriate notice. It's not unusual for us to keep a horse longer. We end up saddle training most of them. All of it is Boone's brainchild."

Beth continued to watch the foals. Several feet away, Alana stood next to Zane, chatting away. The two seemed to be getting along quite well, which surprised Beth. Her friend's cheerful, outgoing nature hid the tragedy which happened eighteen months earlier.

"Do you ride?"

Kell's question grabbed Beth's attention. "I used to ride every day on my parents' ranch near Billings."

"I don't remember you telling me about their ranch."

Shrugging, she focused back on the foals. "Guess we never got around to it. Since moving away, riding hasn't been a priority. I do miss it."

"Monday after work."

She looked back at him, her brows furrowing. "Monday?"

"We'll go for a ride."

Before she could stop it, a grin lifted the corners of her mouth. "I'd like that."

"We'll plan on it. Come on. I want to show you something." Holding out his hand, he took hers, leaving Zane and Alana to their conversation.

Walking around the side of the house, he nodded to a large fenced in area. Following his gaze, her face lit with excitement.

"Oh. They're darling." Kneeling, she reached into the area to stroke one of the puppies. "How old are they?"

"A few weeks. Most of them are spoken for. The mother belongs to Ty. He's keeping one of them."

"I'd love a dog." She lifted one of the puppies, holding him to her chest. "Between my schedule and classes, there isn't much time." Nuzzling his fur, she sighed before placing him back with his siblings.

Rising, she came up within a few inches of Kell. The obvious look of desire on his face slammed into her. Heart racing, her gaze settled on his mouth.

It would be foolish to get involved with anyone right now. Not with her heavy work schedule and amount of homework required by her classes. Add to those her dreadful experience with Freddy, and there were no points in favor of starting something new.

When his hand slid behind her neck, drawing her forward, all the reasons for not getting involved fled. His mouth covered hers, causing all good intentions and reason to flee.

Soft and warm, his mouth made love to hers in ways she'd never experienced. His arms moved around Beth as her hands gripped his shoulders. Chest vibrating, a low moan escaped her lips when Kell deepened the kiss.

Any doubts they'd be good together fled as his broad hands splayed across her back. She knew they should stop. Anyone could see them. Tyler might return from soccer practice, or Zane and Alana could decide to search for them. None of those had her stepping away.

It was Kell who came to his senses first. Raising his head, he rested his forehead against hers. "I've wanted to do that since the day we talked at the high school track."

"I'm glad you didn't wait any longer."

Chuckling, he put a few inches of distance between them. "Yeah?"

"Absolutely, cowboy."

Zane and Kell waved as the women drove away in Alana's red Miata, a present from her parents after earning her associate degree. The sports car fit her. Bright and spirited.

Kell could still taste Beth on his lips. Feel her pressed against his body. His body still strummed with desire for the beautiful woman. Knowing he had to wipe her from his mind, at least for now, Kell withdrew his phone, punching in Del's number.

His chest squeezed, throat thickened at what Del confirmed. It was what Kell expected. Hearing it from the sheriff made it real. The hope Kell held close to his chest slipped away. Ending the call, he stared at the phone.

Zane knew what Kell and the brothers had planned regarding the neighboring ranch they hoped to buy. The look on his friend's face confirmed the news from Del wasn't good.

"Nothing you can do?"

Pacing away, Kell turned back toward him, shaking his head. "Not right now. Del's still investigating the Jernigans. The DEA being involved doesn't make this any easier."

"They could drag the investigation on for weeks or months. Unless…" Zane's voice trailed off as he rubbed his stubbled jaw.

"Unless?"

"Del isn't the only one with friends in the DEA. Let's get coffee and we can talk about it."

Entering the house, Kell headed to the kitchen, stopping at the sound of his phone, not recognizing the number. "Brooks."

"You've got to come get me."

"Who is this?"

"They're trying to kill me. I don't know how long I can hide from them."

"Cliff?"

"There was no heart attack."

Catching Zane's attention, Kell turned on the speaker. "Cliff, are you still inside the hospital?"

"No. They're searching for me. I'll let you know where to find me when you get closer to Dallas."

"Cliff. It's Zane. Do you have food, shelter?"

"I'll make do. Just come…" His voice grew faint as the call ended.

"Damn." Kell called Cliff back. The phone rang without being answered.

"Probably a burner."

Lips drawing into a firm line, Kell slid the phone in his pocket. "Where would he get one?"

Starting the coffee, Zane leaned against the kitchen counter. "You know Cliff. He always carries at least two. The man's a genius at finding what he needs."

"We have to help him."

Zane poured each of them coffee, handing a cup to Kell. "We can leave today, after we've spoken with the Macklins."

Blowing across the top of the coffee, Kell took a few sips, thinking of the call from Cliff. "There was something in Cliff's voice..." Setting down the cup, he pulled the phone from his pocket.

"Hello, this is Kellen Brooks. I'm a close friend of a patient, Clifford Walker. May I speak with someone who can give me an update on his condition?"

"A friend. Not a relative?"

"I'm his emergency contact and responsible for handling his health needs after discharge."

"All right, Mr. Brooks. Let me get someone for you." Less than a minute passed before another woman's voice came on the phone.

"Mr. Brooks. This is Doctor Lang. What can I do for you?"

"Checking on Cliff Walker's progress. How's he doing?"

"He's doing well."

Brows drawing together, Kell shot a look at Zane. "So you've seen him recently?"

"Just came from his room. If all goes well, he may be able to go home by the end of next week."

"I'm not doubting you, but I received a call within the last fifteen minutes from Cliff. He sounded agitated. Wanted to leave the hospital."

"That is odd. I can assure you he is resting peacefully. In fact, the patient who shares the room complained about him always sleeping." She chuckled. "He has no one to talk to when Mr. Walker is asleep. Call Monday and we'll know more about his discharge."

"Thank you, Doctor Lang. I'll call first of the week."

Jaw tight, Kell pocketed his phone. "He's been asleep in his room for a while."

"Not a chance."

"According to the doctor, she was just in his room and Cliff was asleep."

Zane rubbed the back of his neck. "Medication?"

"Maybe." Kell thought of the two FBI agents, and his doubts increased. "But there may be more going on than we've considered."

Chapter Eleven

Kell was restless. Saturday night and nowhere to go. The Macklins were at Grace and Thorn's house for dinner. He and Zane had turned down Grace's invitation to join them. Leftover chicken and biscuits made up their meal.

Afterward, Zane headed to his room, intending to call his DEA contact. Neither expected the man to do much except provide information on their options for going forward with an offer on the Jernigan ranch.

Kell sat at the desk in his room, punching keys to bring up the file he'd created on Colonel August Hayward. Reading through what he and the men in his former unit had compiled, he debated whether to share it with Rhodes and Sparrow.

Somehow, the FBI agents had discovered what he and his men had learned about Hayward's involvement in moving illegal drugs across the western half of the United States.

Kell had been quietly compiling evidence over his last two years of active duty. He, Zane, and Kyle Foster, who'd been killed in South America, had an appointment to present a report to Hayward's commanding officer after returning from their ill-fated mission.

The comments by Rhodes and Sparrow had Kell convinced the colonel knew about the report. The contents would end his career and place him in prison for years. Could Hayward have orchestrated the deaths of the men in Kell's unit to protect himself? Kell no longer believed the idea implausible.

Opening a drawer, he extracted the card Rhodes had given him. Staring at it for several minutes, he tossed it aside before heading to Zane's room. Knocking, he entered when the door opened.

"I think we should hand over what we learned about Hayward to the FBI agents I told you about."

Sitting on the edge of his bed, Zane motioned for Kell to take the chair. "Why not Hayward's commanding officer as we'd first planned?"

He explained his theory someone had leaked the nature of their request to Hayward, prompting the colonel to change the South American extraction orders. The change resulting in the deaths of four of Kell's men.

"We've already decided we're in no position to pursue this ourselves, Zane. Handing over what we've learned to the FBI makes sense. They have the resources to continue what we started."

"Why the FBI? Why not the DEA?"

"A good question. We can ask the agents when we meet with them."

Zane glanced around the sparse room. Three years ago, he would've insisted they go after Hayward themselves. Not only for his role in moving drugs west of the Mississippi, but for any part he played in the deaths of the five men from their squad, and injuries to Cliff.

They were now far removed from their roles in Special Forces. Neither he nor Kell were in a position to exact the type of justice Hayward deserved. Zane still felt the burning desire to be involved in bringing the man down.

"We've got to walk away from this, Zane. Neither of us are Rambo replicas. We're two regular men with dreams disassociated with our former military service."

"I want to be at Hayward's trial."

"Hell, man. You'll be a star witness. It's what we can do to bring justice to our fallen brothers."

Fingers laced behind his head, Kell stared at the ceiling, wondering if giving their report to the FBI would result in Hayward's arrest or be filed and forgotten. Was the agency collecting evidence only to bury what they learned?

No answers came to him. Other than Zane, Cliff, and the Macklins, he didn't know who to trust. The list was short. It certainly didn't include any of the DOJ investigative agencies. They had to prove themselves one agent at a time.

Hearing his phone, Kell sat up, noting the time. Three Sunday morning. Nothing good ever happened at that hour.

"Brooks."

"Mr. Brooks. It's Doctor Lang in Dallas."

Wide awake, he straightened. "Do you have news about Cliff?"

"Well, yes. He's missing."

"Missing?" Grabbing his jeans, he shoved his legs inside.

"I'm afraid so. We've searched the entire hospital and can't find him. His clothes are gone, including his wallet and phone."

"How long since you realized Cliff wasn't in his room?"

"A little more than an hour. Security is still searching, but I thought you should know."

"I appreciate it, Doctor."

"Please call us if you hear from him."

"Thanks again, Doc."

Dragging on a shirt, he stepped into the hall, careful not to wake the others. Without knocking, he slipped into Zane's room and closed the door. Turning around, he stared into a Glock 45.

"Shit, man. Put that thing down."

Lowering the pistol, Zane's mouth twisted in a grimace. "In case you didn't know, it's three in the morning. Why the hell are you sneaking into my room?"

"The hospital called. Cliff is missing."

By noon on Sunday, Del had contacted his counterparts in Dallas and several other cities between Whiskey Bend and Texas. None could do anything officially, but as a courtesy, would have their people watch for a man who matched Cliff's description.

Kell had contacted Agent Rhodes minutes after the sun rose to arrange a meeting. The two agents were expected within the hour.

A decision had already been made for the three Macklin men, and Larry Lawson, to be present when Kell and Zane handed over the report. There were to be no misunderstandings about what the FBI would be receiving. Not that it would matter. The FBI had a reputation for extricating itself from the tightest legal agreements.

The meeting lasted less than thirty minutes. It was clear the FBI knew about Colonel Hayward's illegal activities and were gathering as much additional evidence as possible before recommending charges.

"You will most likely be called to testify." Rhodes addressed his statement to Kell and Zane. "Walker, too, assuming he resurfaces."

Leaning across the table toward Rhodes, Kell pinned him with a quelling look. "We want your guarantee Hayward's activities will be exposed, and not end up in some obscure file cabinet. Because if that happens, we will go to the press."

Agent Sparrow's face flushed. "Are you threatening the FBI, Brooks?"

"Not at all. I'm telling you how it's going to be if there's no action against Hayward. Men have died. We aren't going to let this go until the colonel and his associates are held accountable."

Kell held his breath, waiting for Larry Lawson to interject, but the lawyer held his tongue. Shifting to look at him, Lawson surprised him by giving a brusque nod of approval.

Rhodes responded before Sparrow could. "The task force has put too many man hours into this investigation to let it drop, Brooks. Still, I understand your concern. I'm giving you my word this will not be buried." Pulling out a card, Rhodes wrote on the back, passing it to Kell. "My personal cell number. Feel free to call me anytime. In return, I expect you to let me know if Cliff Walker contacts you."

Watching from the front porch, the Macklins, Kell, Zane, and Larry said nothing as the agents left the ranch. A sense of foreboding fell over the group.

"What do you think, Larry?" Arms crossed, Thorn's features were unreadable.

"The report compiled by Kell and his men is comprehensive and compelling. Unfortunately, a final decision won't be up to Rhodes and Sparrow. The task force will make a recommendation. It'll be up to those above them to take action. I can't even give you odds on which way it will go. I will say threatening them with going to the press caught their attention."

Kell grimaced. "It wasn't a threat...exactly."

"Doesn't matter. They got the message." Larry pulled keys from his pocket. "Well, I'd better head home. My wife is preparing an early dinner. Being late isn't an option."

Kell and Zane stayed on the porch as the brothers walked the lawyer to his car. Kell still had a bitter taste in his mouth over the loss of the family ranch. It was irrational to hold Larry responsible for even a portion of his father's betrayal. The bitterness still tasted as fresh as on the day Kell had learned of the sale.

"I'll head out for a while if you want to talk with the Macklins about what's happening with the Jernigans."

Kell shook his head. "Nah. Del will let me know when it's all right to make an offer."

"My DEA contact knew about the kidnapping and cocaine. He doesn't believe Jernigan will be charged, but there's no guarantee at this point. Either way, he said the land can still be sold." Zane clasped Kell on the shoulder. "And you'll be first in line."

"I'm going to head to the high school for a run. You want to come?"

"You go ahead. I feel the pull of the river." Zane rubbed his hands together. "The fish are calling."

Kell's feet hammered the track, his speed increasing with each lap. Two, three, four, with a goal of eight. Keeping up the current pace would allow him to punch out nine laps, assuming his knees held out.

The run did what he'd hoped. Worries about Colonel Hayward's actions, Cliff's disappearance, and the Jernigan property faded away until the only image in his head was of a beautiful woman.

Thinking of Beth brought welcome peace to his agitated soul. He'd be seeing her tomorrow evening for their ride. It wasn't soon enough.

Kell wanted to lay eyes on her now, not wait until tomorrow. Lap seven, eight. His knees and hips were doing fine. No reason to stop. His thoughts went to what he had in his running bag. An extra pair of jeans, extra t-shirt, clean briefs.

Could he do it? Kell knew where she lived. Would his appearance at her door be taken as stalking, or would she welcome him?

Lap nine. Walking one last lap, he exited the track, heading straight to his truck. Gripping his phone, he stared at her number, debating.

Making a decision, he made the call.

"Beth, it's Kell. I'm coming over."

Chapter Twelve

Beth hung up the phone, wondering what she'd agreed to. Kell was on his way over, of that she was certain. He'd given her no time to ask why he wanted to see her before hanging up.

She'd finished her homework an hour earlier, deciding to take a long bath before fixing dinner. Tonight would be an indulgence. Crab and lobster atop a pile of greens with avocado slices, quartered tomatoes, and artichoke hearts, with miso-ginger dressing.

Sipping chilled white wine, she'd been slicing vegetables when the phone rang. Without looking, she'd answered, surprised to hear Kell's voice. Even more stunned when he announced his intention to stop by.

Since then, Beth had hung up a sweater and summer coat, washed the dishes in the sink, and changed from her old hang-around-the-house-outfit to loose pants, tank, and a thin hoodie.

She'd just returned to slicing vegetables when a knock sounded on the front door. Taking one more sip of wine for courage, Beth set down the knife, and answered the door.

"Hey, Kell. I was—" It was all she got out before he pulled her to him, covering her mouth with his.

Her first instinct was to push him away, kick him if necessary. But the insistent, soft warmth of his mouth sent spirals of pleasure from the top of her head to her purple-painted toes. Instead of shoving his shoulders, her fingers dug into them, telegraphing her desire for more.

Lifting her, he kicked the door closed, whirling around to place her back against it. Deepening the kiss, he felt her hands move from his shoulders to the bottom of his shirt. The realization he'd yet to take a shower had him pulling away.

"I need a shower."

"Whaaat?"

"A shower. I just came from the track."

Shoving strands of hair from her face, she took a step away. "Of course. It's, uh...that way." She nodded toward the hall while tugging at her tank top. "There's just one. You can't miss it."

Noting the confusion in her eyes, the cute way she sucked her bottom lip, he bent to place a kiss on the tip of her nose. "Thanks. I won't be long."

Breathing hard, her heart pounding, she watched him until he ducked out of sight, closing the door. Placing a hand to her throat, she forced her body to calm down.

Never had a kiss affected her so much. Freddy's hadn't held the power of what she'd just experienced, which heated her blood in seconds.

Spotting the glass of wine, she grabbed it, finishing the contents before pouring more. It was just a kiss, she told herself as the shower started. Beth continued to tell herself it meant nothing as she sliced the last of the vegetables, hearing the bathroom door open.

Inhaling slowly, exhaling faster, she forced herself to relax. When he rounded the corner, her breath caught. The white t-shirt stuck to his damp skin, emphasizing his sculpted chest and hard abs. The jeans hung low on his hips, ending at gorgeous bare feet.

Letting her gaze move slowly back up to his face, she flushed at the amusement in his eyes. "I, um...did you find everything you needed?"

"Sure did. You have a nice place, Beth."

"Thanks." Picking up her wine glass, her hand shook as she took a sip. A moment later, Kell settled his hands on her shoulders, bending to place a kiss on the sensitive spot below her ear.

"Beth?"

"Yes?"

"Relax. Nothing's going to happen you don't want." Dropping his hands, Kell opened the refrigerator door, studying the contents. "Do you mind if I have a beer?"

"Please help yourself."

Selecting a bottle of craft beer, he removed the cap, taking a long swallow. "Didn't picture you as a beer girl."

Relaxing, she grinned. "I've been known to have one or two. Sarah's the real beer drinker. She can tell you the differences between an IPA, APA, Strong Ale, Dark Lager, and Bock, and the fermenting process for each. I think she took a class at the local community college."

"And what do you prefer?" He took another swallow, his gaze never leaving hers.

"Wine mostly. Sometimes a single malt scotch. I'm not much for the fruity drinks. They give me a headache. Are you hungry?"

"Always." He moved closer, looking over her shoulder. "Is that real crab and lobster?"

"Absolutely. There's plenty. I also made rolls. All I have to do is heat them."

"Homemade rolls?"

"Baking helps me relax. See the foil package on the counter? Go ahead and put it in the oven. The rolls will be ready in a few minutes."

Doing as Beth asked, Kell leaned against the counter, the beer held loosely in one hand. He watched her finish the salad, appreciating the view. She was exquisite, with long legs, a toned body, and just the right amount of curves. And she fit against him perfectly. Kell gave a sharp shake of his head to get his mind back on an unexpected meal with Beth.

Once the salad was assembled in a large bowl, she removed a bottle of what he suspected to be homemade dressing from the refrigerator.

"Hope this is all right with you. It's a miso-ginger dressing."

"Miso? Like the Japanese soup?"

"The dressing uses the same seasonings as the soup."

Taking the bottle from her hand, he twisted off the cap. "Smells interesting."

"Does that mean you'll try it?"

"Works for me. What can I do to help?"

She nodded at the cupboard next to the refrigerator. "There are salad bowls there, and forks in the drawer under the counter. I'll get the rolls."

The meal was excellent, the company even better. Beth captivated him unlike any woman he'd ever known. She could talk about anything, injecting humor often, and insights which made him think. Kell found himself relaxing, wanting to prolong their time together.

They continued talking while cleaning the kitchen and putting away the dishes. Kell found he didn't want to leave, knowing he had no reason to stay.

"I should let you get back to your studies." He took a step toward her, stopping inches away.

"Other than some reading, they're completed."

A grin quirked up one corner of his mouth as he moved forward. "Is that so?"

She took a step back, hitting the edge of the counter. "For now."

"What are your plans for tonight?"

"You know. This and that."

Lifting his hand, he ran a finger down her cheek, his gaze locked on her lips. "Do you want company?" He bent down, brushing a kiss across her mouth.

Did she? Beth struggled with how to answer. Given the short amount of time they'd known each other, the deep attraction to Kell worried her. After dealing with Freddy, she'd made up her mind to focus on work and school, forgoing male companionship.

His growing attention messed with her plans, as well as her mind. The problem was simple. She enjoyed Kell's company. Much more than she should.

"Beth? No problem if you'd rather I leave."

Leave? Despite promises to herself, she didn't want him to leave.

"Stay, Kell." She didn't have time to second-guess her decision before his mouth covered hers.

The kiss was gentle, searching, before passion exploded between them. Crushing her to him, his tongue traced her soft, full lips before plunging inside.

She clung to him, squirming against his body, unable to get close enough. Her hands moved from his shoulders to his back, her movements frantic. She'd never experienced such rampant desire for a man.

His lips left hers to trail a fiery path to the hollow of her neck. Sucking lightly, he continued, burning a sensuous line to her shoulder. Tendrils of pleasure spread outward. Lips parting, knees trembling, she let out a low, guttural moan.

Lifting her, Kell whispered in her ear. "Put your legs around me."

She did as he said, then wrapped her arms around his neck.

Closing the distance to the bedroom, he laid her in the center of the bed. Stretching out beside her, he stroked her cheek.

"If this isn't what you want, tell me now, Beth."

Wrapping a hand around his neck, she drew him to her. "I want this, Kell. I want you."

Beth woke gradually, her body aching in the most wonderful ways. Stretching both arms above her head, she sighed, memories of the night before assailing her. She didn't need to look to know Kell wouldn't be in her bed.

The sun peeked through the blinds, indicating she didn't have much time to shower and get to work. Beth knew she should feel regret at what happened between her and Kell. She didn't.

Rolling off the bed, she rushed through her morning ritual, swallowing a protein drink before heading out. Anticipation seized her, knowing she and Kell would be going on an evening ride around the ranch. It had been too long since she'd been on a horse. If not for her growing feelings for Kell, it would be hard to contain her excitement.

Believing last night was a mistake was an insult to both her and Kell. He'd been incredible. More than she'd ever thought possible. Her experiences in the past had always left her wondering why so many of her women friends raved about their sexual encounters. Beth's history had been less than stellar. Over time, she'd begun to think the fault was hers.

Last night swept away all her fears of inadequacy. Kell's response to her hadn't been that of a man who wasn't satisfied.

Her growing feelings for the handsome cowboy weighed heavy. She didn't want a relationship with anyone, harbored no desire for the complications common when seeing a man. She had little enough time for anything beyond work and school.

Taking the stairs instead of the elevator, Beth was stunned to see Kell and Boone entering Larry's office.

"What's going on, Alana?"

"I don't know. They were waiting when I arrived a few minutes ago."

Settling behind her desk, Beth began tackling the large stack of files, which had appeared since Friday. The first was the draft of a contract to purchase the Jernigan property. The purchaser line was blank. Her stomach sank.

Beth wondered if that was why Kell and Boone were in Larry's office. As if reading her mind, Larry left his office.

"Good morning, Beth."

"Good morning, Mr. Lawson."

"Ah. I see you have the Jernigan contract. Here is what you'll need to complete it." He handed her a piece of paper from a legal pad. "How soon can you prepare the document for signature?"

"Give me fifteen minutes. Should I bring it to your office?"

"That would be fine."

Larry was old school. He always made corrections by hand. Pulling up the form on the computer, she began the update, hesitating to scan Larry's document for the name of the buyers. Unable to put it off any longer, her gaze dropped to the purchaser line midway down the page.

Chapter Thirteen

Kell didn't stop by Beth's desk or acknowledge her in any way when he and Boone left. She'd glanced up in time to see the phone at his ear as they left the office.

She'd expected a big smile of triumph at his dream being within reach. If the sale went through, the Jernigan property would be split fifty percent to the Macklin brothers and fifty percent to Kell.

Instead, his grim expression confused her. She didn't expect Kell to stop at her desk, sweep her into his arms and kiss her. The way he and Boone hurried outside, their ominous looks signaled trouble.

"Please scan this into the Macklin file, plus a copy in Kell's file." Larry handed her the signed contract. "I'll be going over it with the Jernigans late this afternoon."

Absently, she took the document, her gaze still on the door.

"Are you all right, Beth?"

His words pierced the fog in her brain. Feeling her face flush, she set the contract on her desk. "Yes, I'm fine. I'll get this taken care of right away. I assume you want the original for your meeting?"

Larry studied her a moment. "I believe the appointment is at four."

"I'll have it to you in plenty of time. It's not my business, but do you think Mr. Brooks will get his ranch back?"

Larry grinned, then turned toward his office without answering. Beth knew she shouldn't have asked. She'd hoped Kell would've stopped at her desk to let her know about the meeting, but understood why he'd left. They weren't a couple. Friends with benefits? A bleak chuckle escaped.

Beth had never had a friends with benefits relationship, and didn't know how she felt about it. The few serious relationships she'd had were with men who led her to believe they wanted more. Freddy was one of them. Married with children. She cringed at the reminder of her bad decisions regarding men.

Kell wasn't married, yet Beth knew the former Special Forces ranch hand carried a good deal of baggage. He was as unattainable as her other mistakes.

"Beth, you have a call. Do you have time to take it?"

Alana had taken a few days off, turning her desk over to a temp the firm had used before. A nice woman who sorted out calls and the mail, and accomplished little else.

"I'll take it." She picked up her phone. "This is Beth Hutchison."

"It's Mick."

She groaned.

"Meet me for lunch at Doc's at twelve thirty. We need to talk."

Kell leaned against his truck, phone to his ear while Boone waited beside him. He'd been waiting for the call, hoped it would've come sooner.

"Stay where you are, Cliff. I'll come and get you."

"Can't make any promises, Kell. A couple men and a woman have been following me. I don't know if they're here in Laramie, but can't be sure." Cliff knew Kell would understand. He wasn't in Laramie, but at a town real close.

Checking his watch, Kell glanced around at the sense someone watched him. "I'll leave within the hour. Should take me no more than eleven hours. I'll be there by midnight. Are you on a burner?"

"Yeah. I'll be trashing this one after our call. You?"

"I'll pick up a couple within the next few minutes. Don't trash yours until I call you with my new number. Cliff, don't take any chances. You have cash?"

"I'm set."

"I'll call you when I'm a few hours away."

"Sounds good. I should have an address to give you by then." The call ended without Kell having a chance to answer.

Other than keeping watch around them, Boone hadn't moved from his spot by the truck. "I'll go with you."

"You have to keep things up at the ranch. I'll take Zane. We'll pick up Cliff and be back here by tomorrow afternoon."

"I'll buy burners for me, Thorn, and Del. You'll have three ways to reach us if you need help. And you damn well better use them if you require backup."

Kell drove an almost deserted I-25 south toward Cheyenne. It had been two hours since last speaking to Cliff, and calls to his burner phone had gone unanswered.

Worry plagued Kell and Zane. An unknown someone had been following Cliff since he'd snuck out of a Dallas hospital. They knew their friend, and former squad member, was convinced someone was after him. If it had been anyone else, Zane and Kell might've harbored doubts. Not Cliff Walker.

"Have you heard anything more from those FBI agents?" Zane reached into a bag of fries from their last stop, popping several in his mouth.

He knew Agent Rhodes had contacted Kell a few days earlier with what they had, which amounted to nothing. Their lack of progress in bringing charges against Colonel Hayward had disintegrated from surprising to confusing.

Zane and Kell had handed over pages of testimony, including dates and photographs. As Larry Lawson reminded Boone and Kell that morning, the government worked at its own speed, which was just above a slow walk.

The lawyer had discovered the task force looking into the colonel's actions had been together for eighteen months before introducing themselves to Kell. He didn't doubt the detailed report Rhodes and Sparrow received would move the investigation forward, just not as fast as Zane and Kell would expect.

"Nothing more from the agents." Tightening his grip on the steering wheel, Kell checked his rearview mirror again. "What eats at me is they knew about Cliff and his insistence people were after him. His absolute certainty the heart attack was drug induced."

Zane reached into the paper bag again, holding up several fries. "And they did nothing."

"Rhodes insists he requested additional tests to determine if Cliff had been given a drug which induced an attack, but the labs were never completed."

Zane took a long swallow of his soda. "Or the tests were done and the report lost." At Kell's skeptical look, he shrugged. "Happens all the time."

"So you say." Kell checked the rearview mirror again, relaxing a little.

"Hey, man. You disagree?"

"Right now, I believe anything was and is possible." Bright lights came up fast behind them, drawing Kell's attention. "Behind us, Zane."

Setting the food aside, he flicked off his seatbelt and turned around. "Large truck with large grill guard. Brights are on."

"Yeah. Figured that one out."

"They're preparing to ram us." Drawing his .45 from its holster, he lowered the window and leaned out. "If they hit us, cut to the left. I'm going for a tire."

Both knew it would be almost impossible. Then again, Zane was an expert sniper, becoming equally proficient with handguns at close range.

"One, two..." The truck slammed into them on three.

Kell cut left at the same time Zane leaned out the window, aiming at the right front tire. The .45 revolver cracked three times with at least one bullet finding its mark. The truck swerved, the driver fighting to control the vehicle.

"Get us the hell out of here, Kell."

While the other truck fought to stay on the road, Kell accelerated. Before slowing, they'd put several miles between them.

Zane had stayed in position until sure whoever rammed them was no longer a threat. Snapping his seatbelt closed, he looked at Kell.

"How the hell did they find us?"

"We didn't sweep for trackers."

Zane rolled his head, massaging the back of his neck. "Rookie mistake."

"Or it could've been drunk teenagers."

Chuckling, Zane waved the suggestion away. "Not a chance. The driver and passenger knew what they were doing. They just didn't expect any opposition."

Kell continued to scan the highway ahead and behind them. "We locate Cliff, sweep for trackers, and get out of here. Find us an alternative route back. And call Cliff again. We need a location."

Starting with the call to Cliff, Zane waited through several rings, ready to hang up when a breathless voice answered.

"Cliff. We're half an hour out. Where are you?"

He rattled off a location, his breathing hard and laborious. "I'm hiding in the back parking lot of a bar. Place is loaded with bikers. Call me when you're thirty seconds away. I'll meet you on the street."

Zane wondered about the location, but stayed silent. "Stay alert and watch your back, buddy." Ending the call, he began searching for alternative routes north, settling on one which would take them west on less traveled roads.

Assuming there were no problems, Cliff's extraction would take less than a minute. Checking for tracking devices wouldn't take long with three men, but it would have to wait until they were well away from Cheyenne.

"Five minutes, Zane."

"I'll be ready." Climbing over the seat, he shoved their personal belongings out of the way. When the truck rolled to a stop, he'd shove the door open for Cliff. When inside, Kell would power away from the curb.

Similar to most plans, this one didn't take into account one major factor.

"It's ahead on the right, Kell."

Slowing down, he took in the scene. "The place with all the Harleys, and a group of men surrounding someone on the ground?"

"Damn. Didn't expect this." Narrowing his gaze, Zane groaned, recognizing the man being tormented in the circle of bikers.

Rolling to a stop several yards before the lot, Kell kept the engine running. "What do we have as a distraction?" Both men checked their weapons, unsure what they might encounter.

"How about flashbangs?" Zane pulled two from a duffle bag. "I'll toss one behind the group toward the double row of bikes. You grab Cliff and get him in the truck."

Kell shoved his gun into the waistband at the small of his back, and killed the engine. "Works for me. But first, we get close enough to discover what's going on. Let's go."

The two left the unlocked truck, walking together toward the circle of men. No one noticed them, all too busy taunting the man sprawled out on the ground.

"What's going on?" Kell smiled as if he wanted to be included in their fun.

A tall, burly man with long, stringy hair turned toward them. "None of your damn business. Now, get lost."

Glancing around the foul-smelling man, Kell shot a look at Cliff, getting a quick nod in response. Other than a few superficial scrapes and a small amount of bruising, he didn't appear to be in horrible shape.

Out of the corner of his eye, he saw Zane work his way to a perfect spot to lob the flashbang. Turning his attention to the man who'd moved closer, Kell gave the tiniest of nods.

Before anyone figured his intention, he slammed a fist into the man's gut, then executed a perfect roundhouse kick seconds before the flashbang rocked the entire parking lot.

While the others covered their ears, Cliff got to his feet and ran, following Kell to the truck. Zane threw a second flashbang before taking off after them.

Chapter Fourteen

"Get in!" Kell started the powerful Z71 engine as several of the bikers stalked toward them. A few pulled guns, aiming at the truck. "Hold on!"

Slamming the accelerator to the floor, the wheels screamed as the tires spun before gaining traction and shooting the truck onto the street. Kell let out a relieved breath, noting the light traffic aided their escape. Then he looked into the mirror.

A group of Harleys pulled out of the lot, giving chase. The bikes were lighter, more maneuverable than the truck. The lack of traffic had them gaining on Kell until they were yards behind his bumper.

Several shots hit the truck before one bullet shattered the back window.

"This isn't working for me." Zane aimed his .45 and fired several times.

The bikes swerved, one low-sided while another hit a curb, throwing the rider over the handlebars. The others dropped back, giving up the chase to help their fallen friends.

"Clear, Kell." Zane loaded the .45's cylinder with more bullets before shoving the revolver back into its holster.

"Directions would be good."

Zane provided the route to Kell before hearing a deep moan from the back seat. "Are you all right, Cliff?"

"Nothing I can't handle."

"What is it?" Zane turned in his seat to see Cliff massaging his right ankle.

"Twisted my ankle. You have any ice?"

Zane pointed to his go-bag on the floor behind Kell. "There are a couple cold packs in the duffle. A tin of ibuprofen and bottles of water are in there, too."

"Don't know how I let those guys box me in. I'd hung up from our last call, turned around, and at least a half dozen of them had moved to within a few feet. The big one Kell took down accused me of being an undercover narc. Do I look like a narcotics officer to you?" Cliff's mouth twisted into a grimace as he placed the ice pack on his ankle. "Damn glad you showed up. Not sure I could've taken them all out by myself."

Chuckling, Zane opened a bag of dried fruit, taking out a piece to hold it up. "If you weren't already flat on your butt, you might've had a chance." Popping it into his mouth, he returned his attention to their route home.

"Give me some of that." Holding out his palm for Zane to fill, Kell chewed the dried fruit.

It had been a long time since he'd executed a roundhouse kick. The impact had sent splinters of pain from his hip to his toes. It had been a miracle he hadn't fallen on his face. He checked the mirror, seeing Cliff open the bottle of ibuprofen.

"I'll take a couple of those, Cliff."

Tossing them in his mouth, Kell took several swallows of water, looking at Cliff in the mirror. "Why'd you leave the hospital?"

Another low groan came from the back as Cliff placed his leg with the wounded ankle on the seat. "They were watching me."

"Who?"

"Don't know exactly, Kell. A couple men and a woman, but they never came into my room together. Took turns. Always dressed in hospital garb. My guess is they thought I was too out of it to notice. They're why I made the first call to you. I'd planned to hang up and sneak out, but the doc came in to check me out, and not in a good way."

Kell didn't respond to the intended joke. "Did you recognize any of them from Fort Lewis or anywhere else?"

"Nope. They wore civies, so it's a little hard to be certain. The woman, though..." Cliff's voice trailed off as he pictured the tall, slender woman, with slim hands and cold eyes. "The woman might be someone we knew at the base. Nothing about the men seemed familiar."

"Describe the woman," Zane asked.

"About five-foot-nine. Reddish brown hair worn in a bun of some type. Ruddy complexion, and cold, black eyes. They were the strangest set I'd ever seen. Reminded me of some of those old horror movies we watched as kids. Cold eyes and cold-blooded is the way I'd describe her."

Zane checked the route again before looking up. "What about the men?"

"One was about my height, the other maybe five-nine. No facial hair on either of them. The taller one had brown hair cut high and tight."

"Military cut?" Kell asked.

"Yep. The other man had longer, blond hair. I never got a good look at either of their eyes. The tall one had big, boney hands. I remember because he gripped the top rail of the bed to stare down at me. There was a tat of a knife and rose on his left hand. A spook maybe?"

Kell tapped his fingers on the steering wheel. "Not CIA or any of the alphabet agencies. A knife and rose. Doesn't ring any bells with me. You, Zane?"

"I'd have to think on it, but nothing comes to mind."

"My gut tells me they're connected to Colonel Hayward. I'm certain he's aware of the investigation into his activities."

Zane turned toward him. "Why?"

They hadn't examined Kell's suspicions the deaths and injuries during the extraction in South America were due to an order from Hayward. It seemed farfetched. A colonel in the United States Army targeting his own men to keep illegal activities from being exposed. Money and greed were powerful motivators for many people. Few were immune.

"The way the extraction went down. All the men were scheduled to leave on the same chopper. I'd confirmed the order. All we had to do was keep the enemy behind us until the chopper arrived. When it landed, a few men were helped aboard before two men pointed their guns at the remaining members of the squad, ordering them to pull back until the return of the chopper."

Anger drew tight lines on Zane's face. "This is the first I've heard of it."

"At the time, I didn't think too much about it. Except the chopper could've held all of us. We weren't under fire. It would've been an easy operation to load everyone and take off."

Cliff adjusted himself in the seat, taking a quick glance behind them. "When did you first suspect Hayward of being behind the order?"

"Agent Rhodes offered his thoughts the night I met him and Agent Sparrow. He put the nugget of doubt in my head, and I haven't been able to shake it. The more I put the pieces together, the more the scenario makes sense. Hayward learned about what we discovered from someone."

"A member of the task force." Zane's whispered comment was almost too low to hear.

"Right. When the mission to South America came up, Hayward saw an easy way to rid himself of the men who'd discovered his illegal drug activities. Easy enough to accomplish. The deaths would've occurred during a sanctioned operation. Reports would've been filed and the incident forgotten."

Cliff slapped his thigh. "Except we didn't all die."

"Correct." Kell watched the road ahead of them, looking for the turn Zane mentioned minutes earlier. "Four of us made it out."

"So he devised a plan to kill us off. There'd be no trail back to him, leaving Hayward with a clear path to continue bringing drugs into the northwest." Zane scratched the back of his neck. "Not brilliant, but it would've worked if Cliff had died as planned."

"The colonel would've moved on to you and me. I believe the shot fired at me on the Macklin ranch was no accident."

Picking up a water bottle, Cliff took several gulps. "The big question is, how do we stay alive long enough to testify against the sonofabitch?"

Cliff's question burned in Kell's brain mile after mile. They'd stopped twice to get gas, buy food, and change drivers, yet the question still bothered him.

Having Cliff stay at the ranch would put the Macklins in even more danger. With him and Zane living there, they were already in the crosshairs of whoever stalked Kell. Boone had insisted they stay. The idea now seemed ridiculous. His main priority was to stay out of harm's way while keeping the Macklins safe.

Finding another location wouldn't be difficult. There were plenty of rentals in Whiskey Bend. They'd find a three bedroom place, and other than work, hunker down until Hayward stood trial.

"You know it could be months before the task force arrests the colonel." Zane's sobering comment ended his thoughts on a rental. "Staying at the ranch is the best option. Besides, we both work there. I wouldn't feel right bailing on them when there's so much to do. Plus, there's the purchase of your family's land. A lot to do after the sale is final."

Zane had summarized their situation in a few sentences. Cliff's twisted ankle would take time to heal. He had mad computer skills, was a genius at finance, and was an exceptional strategist.

"Yeah. You're right. I just don't know how far Hayward will go to eliminate the threat we pose."

"He'd kill his own mother to secure the money he's making on the drug deals." Cliff reclined in the back seat, his injured ankle on the seat, eyes closed. "We are a major target. Wish I knew how many people he has searching for us."

Zane relaxed his hands on the steering wheel, watching for his next turn. "We know of the three you saw at the hospital. There were two who tailed us on the way to pick you up."

"Yeah?" Cliff sat up straighter. "What happened to them?"

Zane glanced at Kell before replying. "Probably waiting for their truck to be repaired."

Chuckling, Kell watched the sun begin its ascent over the western mountain range. "If they're all connected, that's five. A piece of cake if they all come after us."

Brow lifting, Zane shot Kell a look. "Remember, we're not taking action. All we're doing is reporting what we know, and keeping ourselves out of harm's way."

Kell gave a reluctant nod. Zane's reminder came at a good time. Although the three former Army Rangers had amazing skills, it had been a long time since they were put to the test. The encounter with the men in the truck, and getting away from a group of bikers was child's play when compared to who Hayward might send after them. Kell needed to remember they weren't the same men as three years ago. Staying alive long enough to testify had become their priority.

Watching the sun rise, his mind traveled to Beth. What the hell was he going to do about her? The other night had been spectacular. Leaving hadn't been easy. Walking out of the law offices without speaking to her still ate at him.

Kell should've made time to at least say hello, but Cliff's call changed his plans. When they got home, with Cliff settled at the Macklin ranch, he'd call her. Even if he wasn't ready to start anything serious, he owed her a few minutes on the phone. Just five or ten to hear her voice, get her to laugh. He could use a good laugh.

Chapter Fifteen

"Any word from your *friend*?" Alana leaned against Beth's desk, drinking a smoothie she'd purchased across the street.

Beth saw no point in hiding her disappointment. "No."

"I heard he and Zane had to go out of town."

She lifted her head from the file opened on the desk. "And you're just now telling me?"

"Hey, I thought you would've spoken with him. Plus, work has been crazy the last couple days." Leaning down, she lowered her voice. "Did you hear the Jernigans accepted the offer last night?"

Beth's eyes widened at the news. "That's great. Has Larry told Kell?"

"I know he spoke with Boone. I'm sure he passed it along to the others."

"True. When is it due to close?"

Alana shook her head. "No idea. The Jernigans are anxious to relocate to where Jim's job is located. They're nice people. Simply clueless when it comes to running a ranch."

Beth believed the same. Kell and the Macklins had the skills and financial resources to resurrect the ranch in no time. Excitement rolled through her realizing Kell would be getting his childhood home back.

The joy was tempered by disappointment at not hearing from him. Coupled with Kell not saying anything when he and Boone were in the office, she wondered if he was sending her a message.

"I'd better get back to my desk. Are you all right, Beth?"

Forcing away the letdown, she flashed a half smile. "Of course. Kell is getting his ranch back. I'm happy for him."

Anger and humiliation for getting involved with Kell surged through her. Swallowing hard, Beth had to admit her part in what happened the other night.

She'd welcomed him into her home and her bed. What man wouldn't have taken what she offered? None she knew.

Her growing feelings for Kell had weakened her defenses. Well, along with the way he kissed, the feel of his rock hard body, and his obvious desire for her.

Beth told herself she'd been carried away by her response to his tender ministrations. Never had she been this attracted to a man. The lovemaking had been beyond anything she'd ever experienced. She could still feel tingles from his kisses, his gentle touch, the heart stopping affection in his gaze.

Hearing Larry's voice, Beth shook off the sensations, forcing herself to concentrate on the work before her. Stopping at her desk, he set down a file.

"The offer on the Jernigan ranch has been accepted. All the details are in the file."

"I'll take care of everything, Mr. Lawson."

"Thank you, Beth. It seems Kell will get his ranch back after all. Along with some partners, of course. If you see him, let Kell know I'm pleased it turned out this way."

She wouldn't tell him they hadn't spoken since he'd been in the office a few days earlier. "I'll do that."

Opening the file, she scanned the final agreement. The Jernigans had accepted the offer with just one stipulation. They wanted to close as soon as possible.

It didn't take long to enter the agreement details into the computer. Closing the file, she felt an odd sense of peace. No matter what happened between her and Kell, he'd have his ranch, the dream he'd kept his entire life.

The rest of the day flew by, giving her little time to think about Kell and why he'd remained silent. Beth preferred running in the morning. Today, though, she'd made an exception.

Reaching the track, she changed, and entered the field. There were four others already on the track. One woman and three men. She'd hoped Kell was one of them, feeling another wave of disappointment when she didn't recognize any of the three men.

Entering the track, she did one slow lap, picking up speed into the second turn. The temperature was perfect, her pace easy. She'd planned ten laps before heading home to a meal of leftover pasta, and whatever movie got her attention. A bleak evening without Kell.

Heading into her third lap, she could sense someone coming up behind her, keeping pace but not passing. The skin on the back of her neck prickled. She picked up her speed, hoping whoever it was behind her would get the message. It didn't happen.

A moment later, the runner caught up, pacing her in the lane to the right. "Are you going to ignore me?"

She knew the voice. Glancing at her side, a smile curved her lips. Kell ran beside her, looking tired and wonderful at the same time. Neither slowed as they continued the run.

"I heard you and Zane were out of town."

"News travels fast. We had to pick up a friend in Wyoming. We were in the Army together. How are you doing?"

"Good. You heard the latest about your offer on the ranch?"

His smile broadened. "Best news I've had in a long time. We hope to close in thirty days. I tried calling you at the office, but you'd left. Drove by your apartment, then decided to take a chance and see if you were here. I'm hoping you'll go to dinner with me to celebrate."

"I'd love to." Her gaze landed on two men standing outside the tall hurricane fence surrounding the track. Neither wore running apparel. "Do you know either of those men?"

Kell followed her nod. They must've followed him from the ranch. "Not by name. Zane and I were followed on our trip. Don't know for certain if these are the same men."

"There's no reason for them to be here unless they're watching someone."

He could hear a slight amount of fear in her voice. "Let's continue our run and see if they stick around. I'm going to call Del."

Punching speed dial, he saw the men step away from the fence, but not leave. Kell felt certain these were the men who'd visited Cliff in the hospital, possibly injecting him with a drug which caused his heart attack. His gaze scanned the parking lot for a woman, not finding one.

"Del, it's Kell. There's a situation at the high school track." Explaining, he gave a satisfied thanks before ending the call. "He and another deputy are heading over. We'll see how those suits handle the arrival of law enforcement."

Continuing their run, it wasn't long before the sound of a siren split the air. Turning in a circle, the men began moving back toward the parking lot, moving faster as the siren became louder. Before they could pull out of their space, Del's SUV pulled in behind them, preventing any retreat.

"This ought to be good. You want to get up close and personal?"

"The sheriff won't mind?"

"We won't get that close. I do want to hear what the men have to say." Taking her hand, Kell led her through a gate toward the group of men.

"As far as I know, Sheriff, there's no law against watching people run. You saying there is?"

Glancing down at the man's drivers license, Del didn't respond to the question. "We had a complaint, Mr. Olsen, and are obligated to check it out. Is there a reason you're at the track?"

"It's none of your business."

Del grinned at the second of the two men before scanning his license. "Mr. Darren Green?"

"Yeah."

"We do have loitering laws in Whiskey Bend. You aren't wearing running gear, there isn't a public event going on, and from what I can tell, there's no reason why you'd be watching the people on the track. Yet here you are. Mind telling me why you've spent considerable time here?"

Chad Olsen locked his hands behind his back, as if trying to restrain himself. "Again, it's none of your business."

"Well, that's too bad. A simple explanation could clear everything up. If you'd prefer, we can go to the station, and you two can drink the county's wonderful coffee while answering questions."

"He can't do that, can he, Chad?"

Not responding, Olsen glared at Del.

"Actually, I can. We found you loitering on school property. It gives me the right to question you. It'd be a lot easier to do it here instead of the station. Your choice."

Del noticed Olsen's left eye tick. "We need our licenses back."

"No problem. I'll run them at the station. Assuming there are no violations pending, you can have them." Del made a show of slipping them into a pocket. "Which will it be, gentlemen?"

"You can run our I.D.s here. No need to go to the station." Olsen wasn't going to let it drop.

"Does that mean you'll answer my questions?"

Neither man responded.

"Deputy Nolen. Please help Mr. Olsen and Mr. Green into the back of the SUV." Del looked at the men, noticing the color rise in their faces.

Kell saw the same. "Beth. I want you to walk back to your SUV and head home."

"Not a chance."

"Excuse me?"

"I'm not leaving."

Cursing under his breath, he took her arm, leading her away. "The situation is deteriorating. Those men aren't going to answer questions here or at the station. Trust me, this is not where you want to be."

"If it's that important to you, I'll stand by the restrooms, but I'm not leaving."

Shouts drew Kell's attention away from Beth and toward the men. Deputy Joe Nolen had drawn his gun as Green reached for something behind his back.

Before anyone else could react, Green pointed the gun at Nolen, firing one shot, missing by a foot. While Joe took cover behind the SUV, Del landed a bruising punch into Olsen's stomach, doubling the man over. Grabbing both arms, Del secured Olsen's hands behind his back, then drew his gun. He aimed at Green's head.

"Drop your weapon and raise your hands, Green."

The man's wild eyes darted between his partner, the sheriff, and the deputy, desperately seeking a means of escape.

"There's no escape, Green. Put down your weapon." Del kept Olsen on his knees, turned away from Green. "We'll go to the station so you can tell me why you're at the high school."

"I can't tell you anything. Olsen is the one with the answers."

"Shut up, Green." Olsen tried to shift his body to see his partner. Del's hand on his back stopped him.

"It's true. I don't know anything except what you've told me."

"I told you to keep your mouth shut!" Olsen's jaw worked, his face red with anger.

Del's breath caught when he spotted Kell make his way behind Green. His friend carried no weapon other than the hand-to-hand combat skills learned as a Ranger. Skills as lethal as any gun.

"You don't want to die today, Green. Just set your gun on the ground, back away from it, and raise your hands." Del caught Joe's attention, giving him an almost imperceptible nod. The longtime deputy knew what his boss meant. If Green raised his weapon, Joe should take him out.

Del's attention shifted to where Kell hid behind a car a few feet from Green. Before he could signal his friend to stay back, Green raised his weapon, aiming it at Del.

A shot cracked in the still air. Eyes wide in disbelief, Green's grip on the pistol loosened, the weapon dropping to the ground. Looking down, he saw the growing circle of blood appear on his shirt. Without another word, he dropped to his knees before toppling to the side.

Chapter Sixteen

Beth slapped both hands over her mouth as the scene played out. Body trembling, she stifled a scream when Green slumped to the ground.

Slumping against the brick wall of the bathroom, her heart pounded a painful rhythm as bile rose in her throat. *Was he dead?* The realization she'd witnessed a man being killed had her gripping her stomach.

"Kell? You all right?"

Del's shouted question hung in the air. What if Kell had been hurt?

"Affirmative. I'll check on Green."

Relief flooded through her. Kell was all right. Shoving away from the wall, Beth took hesitant steps toward the parking lot, needing to see Kell for herself. Before she'd taken a dozen steps, strong arms came around her from behind, dragging her against a muscled chest.

"You don't want to see it, sweetheart."

"Is he..."

"Yes. Paramedics are on their way, but there's nothing they can do." Resting his chin on the top of her head, he inhaled a deep breath, allowing her unique scent of coconut and vanilla to calm him.

Turning in his arms, she reached up, cupping his face. "Are you all right?"

"I'm fine. Glad Joe got off the shot before Green fired on Del." His mouth brushed across hers. "Sorry you had to see it."

"Why did he pull a gun?"

"We'll never know, Beth. My guess is he was in over his head and scared. Chad Olsen will have answers. If he'll talk."

"I wonder why they were watching us." She rested her head against his chest. "I'm a paralegal and you're a rancher. Nothing nefarious."

If he'd been unsure about bringing her into his life, the incident provided the answer. Olsen and Green were after him. He'd never put Beth in danger because of his involvement in bringing a corrupt colonel to justice.

Beth was an innocent. Besides, Kell had already decided tonight he'd end what they'd begun before anyone got hurt. A relationship wasn't in his future. At least not in any future he could see. A broken body and too many terrible memories didn't bode well for building a future with a woman as wonderful as Beth.

"Kell?"

"Hmmm?"

"I'm going home."

"You shouldn't drive after what you've seen. I'll take you home, then come back for your car."

"That's ridiculous. I'm perfectly capable of driving the few blocks to my apartment."

"Then I'll follow you. Once your settled, I'll come back."

Her attention moved to the parking lot where the EMTs loaded Green's body into the van. Their actions made the man's death real. The fact she'd witnessed him slump to the ground from the bullet's impact made her dizzy. Reaching out, she placed a steadying hand on Kell's arm.

"Beth, are you all right?" Instinct had his arm wrapping around her waist, drawing her close. Her face pale, eyes unfocused, Kell chastised himself. "Foolish question."

The woman had witnessed a man's death. Lifting her into his arms, he walked to his truck.

"What are you doing?" Beth's thready voice and weak attempt to get out of his arms spoke to the trauma claiming her.

"You've had a shock. I'm going to place you in the back seat of the truck for a bit." He placed her on the seat, slipping his arms from her.

"I don't need to..." Her voice trailed off at the feel of a broad hand touching her forehead.

"You're skin is damp and clammy. Lean back and close your eyes."

Stroking a hand over her hair, he stayed beside Beth as her breathing evened out. Watching the scene play out in the parking lot, he wondered what they could've done to prevent Green's death.

Frustration wrapped around Kell. One of two men who might have provided answers was dead, leaving his comrade as the one link to who hired them. Two men, played against each other, could produce faster and more accurate results than interrogating one prisoner.

The van's back doors slamming shut drew his attention. His gaze moved to Del's SUV. Chad Olsen's malicious glare locked on Kell from the back seat. Straightening, his hand continued to stroke Beth's hair as he met the prisoner's cold stare.

"Nolen and I are heading to the station with Olsen. There won't be much time to interrogate him before notifying agents Rhodes and Swallow. Do you want to watch the interview?"

So focused on Olsen, Kell hadn't noticed Del's approach. The slip underscored how much his skills had deteriorated during the last three years. He shot a look at Beth, debating what to do.

"Assuming she's up for it, Beth's welcome to come." Del glanced over his shoulder at Nolen, letting his deputy know he'd be right there.

Hearing what Del said, Beth sat up, blinking several times. "I'm fine, Kell. You go with Del. I'll head to my place. Feel free to come over when you're finished."

"I'd rather you come with me to the station and watch the interrogation. Afterward, I'll bring you back here to get your car."

As much as she hated Kell ordering her around, Beth couldn't deny being curious as to how Del conducted the interrogation. She wanted to know why the men were at the high school, and how Kell had become involved in what went down in the parking lot. This might be her one chance. Even their brief friendship had demonstrated how little Kell revealed about himself.

"If you're sure it's all right, Del."

"It's fine with me. But don't pass around what you hear. Don't want the local paper printing something Rhodes or Sparrow might read."

Kell gave a terse, impatient nod. "It's settled. Beth and I will meet you at the station."

The interrogation revealed little. Other than learning Olsen had been ordered to follow Kell, and he'd brought in Green to assist, he refused to name anyone or the reason behind the order. He also pled ignorance at questions regarding Cliff and visits to his hospital room. Del ended the questioning after two hours, making the decision to call Rhodes the following morning.

At ten that night, Kell sat on the sofa in Beth's apartment, cradling a cup of coffee. He struggled with the decision made a few hours earlier.

In the aftermath of the shooting, the decision to end his time with Beth seemed reasonable. Watching her in the cozy kitchen, doctoring her coffee with sugar and cream, he found himself wavering.

Kell liked Beth. A lot. Other than the Macklins and his Army brothers, she'd been the first person in years he could relax around, be himself. Not a single woman intrigued him or held his interest as Beth did.

She was smart, with a great sense of humor and unending patience. He couldn't imagine finding a woman who fit him better in bed. It was as if they'd been made for each other, a thought which scared him more than a little.

"Hey." Sitting down next to him, she reached out, placing a hand on his arm. "You look as if you've lost your favorite horse."

Not responding, he lifted the cup, sipping the lukewarm liquid while not meeting her gaze. Kell had never been in this situation. Caring a great deal about a woman, wanting to be with her while knowing he should end it.

The women he'd seen in the past hadn't meant as much, wanted good times without commitment, the same as him. Beth couldn't be more different than those women.

A man wanted to find a woman like her after all the good times were behind him. Kell wondered about himself. Were the games in his past?

"Kell?"

Setting down the cup, he stood. "I'd better get going."

The concern on her face turned to disappointment, then resignation. "All right." Rising, she moved past him to open the door.

Not moving from his spot beside the table, he faced an internal battle. He should leave, give her up to find a man more suitable, whose past life wouldn't put her in danger.

Instead, he took several slow steps toward her. And instead of walking into the late night, he stopped inches away, staring into the most incredible emerald green eyes he'd ever seen.

Reaching out, he took one of her hands in his, experiencing a rush so soothing and familiar he closed his eyes. Kell had never faced a more difficult decision. Not in the Army, and certainly not in his personal life. The decision became easy a moment later.

"Don't leave, Kell."

Kell's warm hand stroked lightly down Beth's naked back and hips. The sun's rays shown through the thick, wood blinds, reminding him he needed to leave for the ranch. Still, he lingered.

After making love three times during the night, he wanted her again. This depth of desire hit him as a blow to the chest. It had been a rare occurrence when he'd spent the night, or allowed a woman to stay with him. The lingering, the craving for this one woman was new.

Lowering his head, he trailed kisses down her spine. He didn't want to leave the warmth of her bed and body. The knowledge sobered him.

He'd been prepared to walk away, to move her to his past, the same as every other woman he'd dated. The idea of never seeing her again caused a sharp pain to pierce his chest.

Placing one more kiss on her shoulder, he slid from the bed. He had a long list of chores at the ranch. And there remained the decision regarding Beth. He felt as if he faced two doors.

One would lead him on a path similar to where he'd always been. Meaningless relationships with women he'd forget within hours of being together. He knew it well. A choice where all outcomes were predetermined. It held no surprises, no highs or lows.

The other door would send him on a journey of discovery. It would be a trip he'd shunned his entire life, requiring new and undetermined adventures. He'd never failed at anything. The second door held no guarantees, failure being a real possibility.

Dressing, he picked up his shoes and moved to the bedroom door.

"Kell?"

He'd almost made it. Walking back to the bed, he sat on the edge, brushing long strands of blonde hair from her face.

"Are you leaving?"

Bending down, he kissed her cheek. "I have work to do at the ranch." *And a great deal of thinking to do.*

Rolling over, she stared up at him with a sleepy smile. "Thank you."

His brows drew together as he thought of what he might've done to deserve her thanks. "For what?"

"Staying the night. I was afraid you would walk out. Maybe for good."

The insight startled him. Hearing her say what he'd been thinking brought more confusion to his already clouded thoughts.

"I'd never just leave. When this is over, I'll let you know my reasons. You'll never have to wonder why." Brushing a kiss across her lips, he headed back to the door. "Keep alert and watch your back. Call me if you suspect anything, Beth."

Those parting words were the last she heard before the door clicked shut behind him.

Chapter Seventeen

When this is over.

Beth couldn't get the words out of her head the rest of the week. Kell hadn't called, the longest period of time they hadn't spoken. She reminded herself he worked on a ranch, and this time of year meant a long list of chores. It was easier and less painful than believing he'd lost interest.

She'd missed one of her morning runs before resuming on the hope of seeing Kell. He hadn't shown. Beth considered calling him, then shook off the impulse. He had her number and would get in touch when he had time.

"What are you doing tonight?" Alana leaned against the cubical wall, keeping an eye on the reception area.

"Haven't thought about it." Which wasn't true.

It was all she'd thought about since waking before sunup. The problem was all her ideas for Friday night included Kell, who hadn't contacted her since the incident at the high school.

"Not seeing Kell?"

"Doesn't seem that way." Letting out a sigh, she turned her chair to look up at Alana. "I haven't heard from him all week."

Alana now understood her friend's glum mood the last few days. Beth would never admit how she'd fallen fast and hard for Kell Brooks, but Alana knew the truth.

"You know how it is on a ranch. Animals get sick, equipment breaks down, fences have to be checked. The work never ends. I'll bet he's been crazy busy."

"Maybe. Probably."

"I'm certain of it. What we need to do is get you away from the office and your studies. We'll get dinner, then see who's playing at Wicked Waters. You know Kull always has good music on Fridays. I guarantee your mood will be better by the time you arrive at your apartment."

"I don't know..."

"What else will you do? Wait, I know. You'll go by Doc's to get takeout, eat alone, and watch one of the many movies on your streaming service. Besides, you'll be doing me a favor. I'm bored, have no plans, and don't want to go to Wicked Waters alone."

"Sarah Mae is always there on Fridays. You could sit with her."

"You mean Sarah Mae plus one. She always has some new man hanging on her every word. I won't be a third wheel if you come with me."

Sitting on her sofa eating takeout while watching some random movie sounded awful. More so because she'd have nothing to keep her mind off Kell. She'd wonder what he was doing or if he was out with someone else. Those thoughts would drive her nuts.

Logging out of the computer and retrieving her purse from a drawer, she stood. "You're right. I'd much rather spend an evening with you than being alone at my place."

Instead of driving, the two walked to Doc's, stopping several times to look into store windows. One in particular caught their attention. A new boutique carrying trendy clothing, jewelry, purses, and other accessories similar to what they'd find in Missoula.

Deciding to come back during one of their lunch breaks, they continued to Doc's. A few tables were still available when they arrived. Both knew what they wanted, and before long, they were sipping wine and eating pasta. Finishing a shared tiramisu, they thanked Doc before walking outside.

Alana touched her stomach. "I'm stuffed. The tiramisu was great."

Beth nodded, feeling better than she had in several days. "Everything Doc serves is great. Glad we decided to walk."

They could hear the music pouring from Wicked Waters a block away. Stopping just inside, their gazes scanned the already full interior for an empty table.

"There's one in the corner by the bar, with two people and four chairs. Maybe they'd share." Alana nodded in the direction.

"We can give it a try." Beth went first, winding her way between tables. As they approached, Alana grabbed her arm.

"Isn't that Zane with the woman at the table?"

Beth took a closer look at the man. "You're right. I'm sure he'll be willing to share."

Taking another step forward, she came to a halt when another man and woman left the dance floor, taking the empty seats at Zane's table. Heart stopping, she began to back up.

"What's wrong?" Alana shifted to look around Beth. "Oh, no."

"Yeah." Beth's gaze locked on Kell, then moved to a stunning redhead. Pulling out her chair, he took a quick look around, freezing when he spotted Beth. "Let's go."

Whirling around, the two hurried toward the entrance. Stepping outside, Beth didn't slow down as she continued in the direction of the law offices. She felt sick...and foolish.

Memories of Freddy assailed her. She'd become physically ill when learning he was married with two young children. Her stomach churned now in a similar way. Slowing down, she sucked in a slow breath.

"Are you all right?" Alana's concerned voice should've given her comfort. Instead, pain and humiliation wrapped around her as tight as a vise.

"Not right now, but I will be."

"What can I do? Do you want me to go back and punch him?"

Beth looked at Alana, and couldn't stop the peel of pained laughter. "No, but thanks for the thought. I just need to get home."

"That's the worst thing you can do. Come on. We're going to the bistro. It's close and has fabulous coffee."

Alana refused to allow Beth to sulk alone. Taking her arm, she turned them in the direction of the bistro.

Kell excused himself from the table, doing his best to wind his way between tables to reach the door. Stepping onto the sidewalk, he searched for Beth, a sinking feeling tightening his stomach.

Cursing under his breath, he walked to the curb, continuing to look for her. He'd meant to call her all week, but work claimed all his time. Then another hiccup changed his plans.

An ex-girlfriend of Zane's arrived unexpectedly with her sister. It had been years since they'd seen each other, longer since they'd dated. They begged Zane to show them around town, and he, in turn, begged Kell to join them. Feeling trapped, and owing his friend, he agreed to join them. He hadn't expected the guilt settling over him.

Twice, he'd tried to call Beth, inviting her to meet them at Wicked Waters. Twice, he'd been interrupted. Standing in the middle of the street as he searched for her, Kell kicked himself for not trying harder to reach her.

The look on Beth's face when she'd spotted him with another woman gutted him. She'd taken off as if fire nipped at her heels. He couldn't blame her. Cursing himself, he walked back toward the saloon while gripping his phone. She didn't answer. Not his first call or the second.

Rejoining Zane and the women, he tapped fingers on the table, trying not to let his restlessness show. When the girls agreed they were ready to find someplace to eat, Kell took Zane aside to explain about Beth.

Giving a brief wave when Zane escorted the women down the street, he jumped into his truck. Suspecting Beth had gone home, he was stumped to see her SUV missing from its designated spot.

Pulling out his phone, he tried to reach her again, leaving a message for her to *please* call him back. He thought about where she might be. Remembering Alana had been with her, he began driving up and down the few short blocks of downtown Whiskey Bend.

Entering the last street, Kell noticed the bistro he and Beth had visited the first time they'd been out together. The night Agents Rhodes and Sparrow had tracked him down. Grimacing in disgust, he took a quick look through the glass, slamming on his brakes.

Beth and Alana sat at a table in deep conversation, neither smiling. Parking, he debated what to do next.

Interrupting them would cause a scene and anger Beth more. Giving her time wouldn't be much better. Her anger would fester, blowing up well out of proportion. The best option would be to wait at her apartment until Beth got home.

Backing out of the space, he drove straight to her complex, hoping she'd listen to his explanation.

Beth stopped a few feet from her door, cocking her head. A lone light shone from inside. She couldn't remember turning on a lamp or leaving a light on when she left before work.

Hesitating a moment, she tried the knob, finding it locked. Feeling a little better, she used her key, shoving the door open enough to look inside.

She could see about half the living room from her spot outside the apartment. A lamp shone on a side table. Still confused, she stepped inside.

"Hello, Beth."

She yelped, jumped back, and whirled toward the kitchen. A hand flew to her chest. "Kell. What are you doing here?" Remembering what she'd seen at Wicked Waters, she threw her purse on the sofa, and stomped toward him. "What happened to your date?"

Holding up his hands, palms out, he walked into the living room. "It wasn't a date."

"Right. Well, it doesn't matter. We've never dated either."

Turning away, she stalked down the hall to her bedroom, slamming the door. Muttering to herself, she tore off her work clothes, replacing them with sweatpants and a long-sleeved t-shirt. Grabbing a brush, she pulled it through her hair, cursing when she encountered a few tangles.

How dare Kell try to explain away what she'd seen as nothing. The situation was no different than the night they'd met. If she hadn't entered the saloon, he probably would've ended up taking the gorgeous redhead to a light dinner at the bistro.

Placing both hands on the vanity, she drew in a slow breath, willing her anger away. No matter how intense their short time together had been, they'd never discussed being exclusive. He could spend time with other women, no matter how much pain it caused.

A few weeks of seeing each other didn't amount to much. He didn't owe her an explanation, shouldn't be pressured to provide answers. She refused to be *that* woman.

A knock on her bedroom door had her straightening.

Did she want to speak with Kell or send him away? It was like choosing to be strong or acting the coward.

Striding across the room, she pulled the door open. Crossing her arms, she met his unyielding gaze, keeping her voice even. "You didn't need to come by. What you do with your time is your business."

A slight grin tilted up the corners of his mouth.

Dropping her arms, she walked past him, heading to the kitchen for a glass of wine. Filling the glass, she took a sip.

"Do you mind if I make coffee?" Kell entered the kitchen, grabbing a cup and coffee pod.

Sweeping her hand in the air, she leaned against the counter. "Be my guest."

This time, he stifled a grin. Waiting for the coffee to finish, he snagged the cup, turning to face her.

"Her name's Mary Jane. The other woman once dated Zane."

"Mary Jane? Did you pick her up at Wicked Waters?"

"No, Beth. You're the only woman I've picked up in a long time."

Eyes wide, she glowered at him. "You did not pick me up."

"What would you call it?"

Glancing around, she tapped a finger against her lips. "I picked *you* up?"

Throwing his head back, he roared with laughter.

"Well, I did."

Setting down his cup, he closed the distance between them, dragging her against him. "And you can pick me up anytime you want, babe."

Chapter Eighteen

Beth sat at one end of the sofa, Kell at the other. She'd allowed him a few kisses before shoving him away, wanting a better explanation. Both held cups of coffee. He sipped his while she stared into hers.

"I should've made time to call you this week."

Beth glanced up at his words without responding.

"Between a time-wasting meeting with Rhodes, Sparrow, and their boss in Missoula, and the work which had stacked up at the ranch..." Looking at her doubtful expression and raised brow, he started over. "Look, Beth. I'm sorry I didn't call. Especially today when Zane's ex-girlfriend and her sister showed up. He had no warning. Seems his mother still thinks she's perfect for Zane and gave her the ranch's address."

A slight grin formed in an attempt to soften her next question. "Are you saying he forced you to go out with the three of them?"

Setting his cup aside, he leaned toward her. "He didn't force me, but I owe him. I won't go into details. He called in a marker and I fulfilled it. What I should've done was call you to join us. I started to, but the women showed up and we took off."

Kell realized what he'd said, wincing at his words. He never explained his actions, and certainly didn't owe Beth one. They'd never discussed being exclusive. Maybe this was the time to cool things between them.

Anger at Kell vanishing, Beth's mind shifted to the stunning redhead who couldn't take her eyes off him. "Both women are beautiful."

"No arguing that. Both are models, visiting for a few days before returning to New York for scheduled shoots. Zane hinted her profession, and his, was why they broke up. It was hard enough to maintain a relationship while in the Army."

Kell sat forward, dreading what he'd say next. "I think this may be a mistake, Beth."

Her stomach clenched. "A mistake?"

Standing, he paced several feet away, picking his words before turning to face her. "I'm not a relationship guy. I'm not good at it, nor is it something I want. It would be best if we took a break for a while."

Wrapping her arms around her waist, she struggled to answer. Unable to meet his gaze, she sat stone still, her mind going blank.

"Beth?"

Swallowing the pain lodged in her throat, she raised her head to look at him. She refused to plead for him to stay. He wanted out, then she'd accept it and move on.

"If that's what you want."

Summoning all her courage, she rose. Squaring her shoulders, she lifted her chin. Stepping to the door, she opened it while forcing a smile.

"You're a good man, Kell. I'm glad we had a chance to meet."

Closing the distance between them, he lifted his hand, lowering it when she stepped away. "Beth, I..."

Fighting the tears burning at the backs of her eyes, she gave a slight shake of her head. "It's all right. If it's over for you, then...it's over." She drew the door open all the way, motioning for him to leave. "Be happy, Kell."

Opening his mouth to reply, he closed it. Within the space of fifteen minutes, he'd kissed her silly, then ended their relationship. No matter how she tried to hide her feelings, he couldn't miss the pain in her eyes, the confusion in the drawn lines on her face.

Kell shouldn't have said anything until taking time to sort it all out. "Beth..." He had no more words, having already messed this up beyond repair. "Take care of yourself, Beth. You're a wonderful woman."

Finding it hard to breathe, she watched his retreat, his last words hurting her as much as his dismissal.

"It seems I wasn't wonderful enough." Her whispered words carried through the air, but not loud enough for him to hear.

It was for the best, Kell told himself over and over on his way back to the ranch. Relationships had never worked for him. Women expected too much and demanded explanations when he hadn't called within a period acceptable to them. They questioned him when they weren't together, and insisted he account for all his time.

Yet Beth had never chastised him for not calling. Never demanded he account for his time when they weren't together. Instead of approaching him in anger at Wicked Waters, she'd left.

Kell doubted she would've called. It wasn't her style. Unlike some women, she had innate grace, a sense of elegance and pride keeping her actions in check.

He'd been the one to enter her apartment uninvited. She'd been surprised, yet didn't rage at him or demand answers. Being honest, he might not have responded with the same restraint if their situations had been reversed.

Not wanting to face the Macklins and Zane in such a rotten mood, he turned onto a side road taking him to one of his favorite spots. The lake had been a place he'd visited often while growing up.

When younger, he'd ridden his bicycle, then driven the truck he'd purchased as a high school sophomore. On a rare occasion, he'd bring a girlfriend. Kell preferred to enjoy the time alone, staring at the water while watching for the plentiful wildlife.

At tonight's late hour, he found the small parking lot empty. It surprised him. Friday nights had always been a popular time with high schoolers.

Turning off the engine, he sat, making no move to leave the truck. Staring straight ahead, he thought of what happened at Beth's apartment.

Kell couldn't get Beth's hurt expression out of his mind. She'd tried to hide it, forcing herself to conceal the pain. He admired her more than any woman since dating in high school. But there was more.

Bright and beautiful, with a calming presence, he'd been attracted to her the first time they'd shared the track. Knowing she worked for Larry Lawson may have dampened his interest for a short time, but his deep attraction toward her won out.

He'd fought his growing feelings, tried not to think about her, worked to come up with excuses for the erratic beating of his heart when she was around.

It was too soon. He wasn't interested in anything longer than a few weeks. Fitting her into his already tight schedule would require too much work. All were lies.

Kell had already fallen for Beth. Then why had he ended it tonight?

Scrubbing both hands over his face, he cursed the fear which had gripped him in her apartment. Fear had never been a word he acknowledged while in the Army. Nothing stopped him from completing their missions. Certainly not the fear of being wounded or killed.

How could one beautiful, sweet woman achieve what dozens of missions hadn't?

Fear of failing her.

Fear of not meeting her expectations.

Fear of giving his heart to her.

Fear of her rejection.

They were excuses. Justifications which hurt a woman who meant a great deal to him.

Leaving the truck, he took a path along the water's edge. He knew it well. Hiking alone gave him time to sort out his thoughts without life's normal interruptions. Tonight, he wouldn't walk far.

Kell already suspected he'd made a mistake. The hardest decision would be how to reverse what he'd done.

Beth tossed about, kicking off covers, then dragging them back up to tuck under her chin. Her heart hurt, and she had no idea how to stop the pain.

Turning her head, she checked the time. Well after midnight.

Giving up, she sat on the edge of the bed, not knowing what to do next. How had it come to this? She'd never meant to fall in love with Kell, had been determined to protect her heart.

Shoving up, she plodded down the hall to the kitchen. Tea might help. Holding a warm cup while curling up on the sofa had always relaxed her. Maybe a movie she'd seen a dozen times would help her fall asleep.

She'd gone over their conversation a dozen times, trying to identify what she'd said to cause Kell to walk out on what they'd started. Nothing made sense. All Beth could come up with was he'd already made up his mind to end things. The idea increased her heartache.

Stirring a small amount of lime sugar into her tea, she found the controller before curling up on one end of the sofa. Choosing a feel good movie, she settled back.

Instead of the movie taking her mind off Kell, she found herself wondering what Kell was doing. Had he been able to go home and fall asleep as if what he'd done had no effect on her? Of course he had.

Kell had told her stories of falling asleep under the most unlikely conditions during his time in the Army. The experiences gave him the ability to sleep anywhere for short periods of time.

There was so much he'd done and experienced, most of which had no place in civilian life. Still, he'd talked of taking her camping, teaching her fly fishing, and how to read the stars. None of those would take place, at least not with him.

It didn't matter. Beth could learn how to fly fish and read stars on her own. She didn't need Kell or any man to teach her.

Beth thought of the weekend ahead. She'd run at the school, but in the evening instead of the morning. Kell preferred getting there early, right after dawn.

Treating herself to a cinnamon roll and coffee at the bistro sounded good, as did fixing Thai food for dinner. Maybe she'd call Alana, find out if she had plans for the weekend. She knew her friend liked Thai.

Beth remembered she had to register for summer classes. Two would be her limit, taking her another step closer to graduating.

Her mother would expect to hear from her on Sunday. Beth had told her about Kell. For now, she'd keep the fact he'd walked away to herself. She wasn't ready to broadcast her poor choices to her family. Not yet, anyway.

Ticking off her plans caused her eyelids to grow heavy. Maybe she'd sleep for hours, not waking until noon or later.

Whatever it took to forget Kell and the loss of his friendship.

Chapter Nineteen

"We know where she lives and works, Colonel. This may be our last chance to silence Brooks, Talbot, and Walker before it's too late."

Colonel August Hayward paced his office, hands clasped behind his back. It was never supposed to go this far. He'd agreed to help with three shipments of drugs brought in from Afghanistan. Three shipments had turned to six, then twelve. Now they demanded twelve more.

Hayward's offshore bank account had grown to astronomical proportions, as had the risk. They now threatened his wife and children if he didn't continue his work. What seemed a simple way to provide for the future of those he loved had turned into a living nightmare.

It would never end unless he found a way to stop them.

Hayward had already made provisions for his family to fly out of the country. Checking the time, relief washed over him. Their plane would be taking off in less than ten minutes.

His next move would be to neutralize the handpicked men under his command who'd gone along with his illegal actions. The men who'd been with him since the beginning.

It had been a bigger mistake to go after those under his command. Men he'd sent on a mission, then turned it into a killing field. It was a traitorous act, which he knew would cost him his freedom. Perhaps his life.

"Colonel, I need your approval to go forward."

Going forward meant kidnapping Bethany Hutchison, using her to control the three remaining men from the South American operation. He refused to do more harm to innocents.

"I'll have a decision later today."

"But, Colonel—"

"Later today, Major. Stand down until you hear from me."

"Yes, sir."

Waiting for several minutes, Hayward made a call. "Are they gone?"

"Yes, sir. Their plane flew out ten minutes ago. Weather is good, and they should reach their destination by 2400 hours. Will you be following, sir?"

"Not now. Let me know when their plane touches down."

"Yes, sir."

Lowering himself into his chair, Colonel August Hayward opened his personal journal. Picking up the hundred dollar pen his wife had given him for Christmas, he read the engraving.

You'll always be my hero.

Regret, deep and bitter, stuck in his chest. There was a time he may have deserved the sentiment. Years ago, before he'd betrayed his men and his country.

Shoving aside his personal shame, Hayward began to write.

"Kell. Are you ready to ride to the neighbors?" Boone leaned against the stall where Kell wrapped a mare's lower leg after applying a thick layer of salve. When he didn't respond, Boone moved closer. "You all right, buddy?"

He wasn't. Nor was he ready to talk about it to Boone or anyone else on the ranch. It had been three days since walking away from Beth. More than once, Kell had thought of calling her, dismissing the idea each time.

"I'm good. Let me tack up Joker. Ten minutes, max."

Kell had worked from dawn to past dusk, doing all he could to push Beth from his mind. Not because he wanted to forget her. Far from it.

He needed time to get his head straight, decide the best way to approach her. She deserved so much better than what he'd dished out Friday night. Beth refusing to speak with him was a definite risk.

The Macklin brothers waited for him at the start of the trail dividing the two ranches. The Jernigans were out of town, looking for a house near Jim's new job. Larry Lawson had another commitment, but assured them an attorney from his office would meet them with keys to the house.

"You gonna tell us what's going on with you, Kell?" Boone rode beside him, lines of concern etching his face.

"I ended things with Beth."

The muscles in Boone's face slackened, but he remained silent.

"Can't even tell you why. We were talking about something that happened Friday night."

"Zane told me his ex-girlfriend showed up with her sister."

"Yeah. The four of us went to Wicked Waters. Beth saw us there."

"Did she make a scene?"

"Not at all. She left with Alana. Never came by our table." He scrubbed a hand over his face, feeling the weight of what he'd done. "I waited at her apartment until she came home. Beth was upset, but calm. She asked a few questions, the same ones any man would ask if they'd spotted their girl with another guy. Nothing she said set me off. Hell, I don't know what happened." Kell glanced behind him at Thorn and Del, who rode about ten feet behind them, talking between themselves. "I told her it would be best if we cooled things for a while. The look on her face, Boone." He shook his head. "I'll never forget the hurt."

They rode in silence for a few minutes before Boone spoke. "You're having second thoughts."

"Within minutes of leaving her place. What's wrong with me? She's perfect. Why would I let her go?"

"Fear."

Kell could argue he'd faced a lot worse and never felt fear. Except he knew Boone was right. His heart had

169

become involved. Other women had come and gone during his life. One or two he thought he loved. He knew now how wrong he'd been. Not one had touched his heart the way Beth had in a few short weeks.

He choked out a harsh laugh. "Who would've thought I'd live through all those years in Special Forces to come home and be brought to my knees by a woman."

"Don't think you're special. Happens to all men who fall in love."

"Whoa. I'm not in love with Beth." He knew the words were a lie the moment they left his lips.

"Keep telling yourself that. It won't do you any good, though. It's already too late."

"How would you know?" Kell knew he fought a losing battle.

"'Cause I know you, and you've got it bad." Boone leaned over, slapping Kell on the back. "Hey, it's not a bad thing."

"It is if she won't speak to me."

"This happened on Friday. It's Tuesday. Have you tried calling her?"

"No."

"What was that, Kell?"

He gritted his teeth. "No, I haven't called her."

"Maybe it's time you did."

Taking a turn in the trail, the house came into view, ending their conversation for now. Kell had a lot to think about.

Kell and the Macklins didn't look at the house before making their offer. As his childhood home, no one saw the need. What they saw surprised them.

The place looked great from the outside. Better than when his parents sold it and the ranch. The Jernigans had applied a fresh coat of paint, repaired the roof, installed new windows, and spruced up the yard with new landscaping.

Pulling out his phone, he snapped a few pictures while waiting for the attorney to arrive. Maybe he'd send a couple to his mother. Something to think about.

Ground tying their horses, the men congregated on the wide, wraparound porch. Kell would move in when the sale finalized.

His feelings about leaving the Macklin ranch were bittersweet. He'd grown accustomed to the constant buzz of activity inside the house, as well as the lively discussions at dinner. It would take a while to adjust, but having his home back was worth it.

The house and three hundred acres around it would be his. The remaining acreage would be deeded to the partnership. Thorn and Del were already talking with local developers regarding turning part of the land into lots for purchase. Done right, the sales could provide a substantial infusion of capital into their horse breeding program.

The four men turned at the sound of tires crunching on the gravel drive. A white truck Kell didn't recognize pulled to a stop in front of the garage. He did recognize the woman driving it.

Gut clenching, he shot a look at Boone before descending the steps to the yard. His first thought was Beth had to know he'd be here. The second was how spectacular she looked.

"Hello, Beth. Thanks for coming."

"Kell. Is everyone here?"

"All four Macklins and me. Do you have the key?"

She held it up, taking the porch steps to join the others. Exchanging greetings, Beth unlocked the front door.

"Gentlemen. I'll bet you're anxious to see inside."

Del placed a hand on Kell's shoulder. "Not as much as this guy."

"Then I won't make you wait." She stood aside as the men entered.

Kell was the last to cross the threshold into the living room. His breath caught at the changes.

"My understanding is the Jernigans refinished the floors, baseboards, cupboards, and doors. Painted the walls. Installed new appliances and granite countertops in the kitchen." She stopped beside the fireplace. "I'll let you look for yourselves."

Kell could look anytime. What he wanted to do was take Beth aside, apologize, ask for another chance. Now wasn't the time. Although he might be able to take a different approach.

While the others moved to the other rooms, he hung back, waiting until they were alone. Before he could implement his plan, she walked past him to follow the others. She didn't spare him even a slight glance when leaving to follow the others.

The snub bothered Kell more than he would've thought, underscoring how much his walking away must've hurt Beth. Shoving his hands into his pockets, he spent a little more time in the kitchen before taking the stairs to the second floor.

The Jernigans had updated the rooms, as they had the living room and kitchen. He knew the others were still downstairs, so he took his time.

His old room was Kell's first stop. The trophies were long gone, packed in a box and stored in a shed a few miles away. The same with a few other items, such as pictures his mother boxed for him.

Without the furniture, it could've been any room in any house. Any trace he'd spent most of his life had been washed away with new paint and refurbished floors.

The other rooms were the same, even the master bedroom. The paint was neutral, the floors the original wood. His mother's carefully chosen and cared for antiques were gone, replaced with glass and chrome furniture. This would become his room.

"Is it what you expected?" He turned to see Beth standing in the doorway, her gaze moving over the furnishings. "I hope you aren't disappointed."

Kell thought it an odd comment. "I had no expectations, so no disappointment." Walking toward her, he let out a calming breath. "Beth, about Friday."

Waving a hand in the air, she gave him a too bright smile. "Not to worry. I'm fine and moving on."

It wasn't what he wanted to hear. "I wondered if maybe—"

She cut him off before he could finish. "You wanted it to be over and it is. I wish you nothing but happiness. I'd better check with the others. I'll need your signatures on the inspection form before we leave."

Taking a long look at her, he nodded. "Sure, Beth. Whatever you want."

Chapter Twenty

Kell drank a third cup of coffee while watching the financial channel early Wednesday morning. Yesterday hadn't gone well. Granted, he hadn't been prepared to see Beth, and should've put off what he had to say for another time. Her cutting him off was for the best.

Picking up the appraisal Boone had received the day before, he studied the properties deemed comparable to his family's ranch. Two were on the south side of Whiskey Bend, and the third to the north. All were familiar to Kell.

He couldn't dispute any of the choices. One had been remodeled, making it the closest match to the home he'd be moving into soon. Reading through the entire report, his gaze latched onto the current value. Not surprising, it matched their offering price to the penny.

Hearing his phone, he reached into a pocket to see Brent Nance's name. "Hey, Brent. How are you?"

"Great, Kell. I wanted to let you know Larry Lawson called about the ranch. The Jernigans would like to close earlier than in the contract. We have everything needed on our end. So I'm clear, you're under no obligation to close sooner."

"I'm good with closing whenever they want. Let me talk to the Macklins and get back to you. What date are they looking at?"

"This week, if possible."

Kell sat up. "That is fast. You have my money in your bank."

"The Macklins, too," Brent added. "It's really up to the bank to prepare the documents. Talk to the Macklins and we'll go from there."

"Thanks, Brent. I'll get back to you soon."

Excitement rolled through him. If the deal finalized this week, he could start moving in as early as Saturday. He and the brothers could plot out new corrals and the new barn they'd discussed. Thorn and Del could show the property to one or two of the developers. All of this while keeping up with the work around the Macklin ranch.

He welcomed the tight schedule. Sixteen hour days sounded good right now. Whatever he had to do to keep Beth from infiltrating his thoughts.

Making quick calls to each of the Macklin brothers, Kell got back to Brent within the hour. "We're ready as soon as the papers are signed. Should I call Larry?"

It still felt odd to talk about the attorney he'd sworn never to work with again. Then he'd learned it had been Larry who spoke to the Jernigans about an offer. Someday, Kell would find a way to thank him.

"I'll call them. When are you available to sign?"

"Thorn and Del can stop by anytime. Boone and I will make ourselves available as soon as the paperwork is ready. Thanks, Brent, for all your work on this."

"My pleasure, Kell. Your father treated you wrong. I'm glad I could play a small part in you obtaining your dream."

Hanging up, Kell thought of all the people who'd been involved in making the sale possible. Brent, Larry, the Macklins. The brothers didn't have to use their savings to purchase the ranch. He knew it would end up being lucrative for all of them. Still, he knew they had other choices. Unlike his father, his lifetime friends had chosen him.

Beth amended the documents required to finalize the sale of the Jernigan property. Staring at the names, her gaze hovered over one in particular. Kellen Brooks would soon be able to reclaim his home and a good portion of the land where he'd grown up.

As happy as she was for him, a profound sadness claimed her. Beth thought she'd done a good job hiding her feelings during the walk-through a few days earlier. Seeing him for the first time since he'd walked out forced all the air from her lungs.

Beth missed him so much more than she'd thought possible. Perhaps because she loved him. She'd thought he might have similar feelings for her. How wrong she'd been.

Kell had been clear he wanted to speak with her when they were at the house. Hearing more reasons why they didn't belong together. Her fragile heart could take just so much, and more of his excuses would be pushing the limit.

She'd never thought going into Wicked Waters would signal the end of their time together. The experience turned out to be a hard lesson. Never again would she allow herself to become attached or open her heart in such a short period of time.

Beth recalled the same promises made after learning Freddy was married. How had she forgotten them so quickly? She wouldn't make the same mistake again.

"How are the Jernigan documents going, Beth?"

"Almost finished, Mr. Lawson. I'll bring them to your office within the next ten minutes."

"By the way, I want to thank you for meeting the Macklins and Kell at the house. I'd thought one of the other attorneys would be available, but..." He shrugged and walked away, but not before she'd seen a glint of mischief in his eyes.

Did he know about her and Kell? Could the meeting have been his way of getting them in front of each other? Snorting a chuckle, she shook her head. A fanciful notion. Larry Lawson was too busy to waste his time matchmaking.

The only person who knew what happened was Alana. Beth hadn't even told her mother. It had been a short relationship. Too short to have fallen in love. Her mother and father had known each other for years before marrying. The older woman would never understand how Beth could've lost her heart after a few weeks. Beth didn't understand either.

Hitting the print button, she walked to the front. Counting five copies, she delivered them to Larry's office, glad he wasn't present.

"Beth. You have a call." Alana lowered her voice. "It's Mick. I can tell him you aren't available."

Pausing for a few seconds, she grinned. Of all the people she didn't want to talk to, Mick stood at the top of the list. "That would be great, Alana. Thanks."

"Also, you have a couple messages. Oh, and your voice mail is full."

Lifting a brow, she took the messages, frowning. "Who is Jeffry Gaines?"

"He owns the photography studio close to Doc's."

"Any idea why he'd call?"

Alana chuckled. "My guess is word travels fast."

"Word?"

"You and Kell breaking up."

"Impossible. You're the only person I've told."

One of Alana's shoulders lifted in a shrug. "Check the other message."

Her face scrunched in confusion. "Who's Jim Dennigan?"

"He owns the truck dealership at the north end of town. Jim's rumored to be a real catch."

"So both messages are personal?" Beth couldn't ignore anyone asking for legal services.

"If they aren't, they'll call back."

Agreeing, Beth balled up the messages, tossing them in Alana's trash. "Do you feel like going out on Friday? Maybe hit Wicked Waters again."

"Sure."

Returning to her desk, Beth felt her mood lighten. A night of good music, dancing, and a gourmet burger with garlic fries would do her good.

Colonel August Hayward dismissed the major who'd been hounding him about Bethany Hutchison. Before long, the man wouldn't accept his excuses and try to contact the cartel himself. It would be a waste of time.

Young and greedy, with nothing to lose except his freedom, the major had an overabundance of arrogance and little regard for his life. He didn't fear the cartel. A grave mistake when partnering with men who lacked a conscience and held even less regard for human life.

Hayward knew firsthand what could happen if one ended up on the cartel's bad side. It's the reason his wife and children were safely tucked into a lavish home in Montenegro with new identities. He doubted the cartel would search for them. If they did, and discovered their location, Hayward had already made arrangements for them to move to Moldova, then on to Vanuatu.

Other than his wife and children, he had no family. Neither did his wife.

Removing his journal from the hidden drawer in his desk, the colonel continued with his detailed activities with the cartel. Names, dates, and locations were added, as well as other information useful to those investigating him.

A few more days and everything would be in place. He had three options going forward. Take his own life. Give himself up. Disappear. Hayward was too selfish to end his life. Living the rest of his life in a federal prison would be a death sentence. There were enough cartel members incarcerated to complete a kill order from numerous cartel leaders.

Hayward wanted to live, watch his children grow to adulthood, and spend his aging years with his dear wife. A woman who knew nothing of his illegal activities.

Setting down the pen, he checked the time. An hour had passed. It wouldn't be long until everything he knew would be entered in the journal. Three copies would be made, then he'd be free to join his family.

Kell finished his ride along the fence line between the two properties, finding the simple task helped to keep his mind off Beth.

Boone had made an appointment for the two of them to meet with Larry at a coffee shop near his office. Thorn and Del had already done their part. Once all four signed, the documents would be filed and keys would be provided no later than Saturday morning.

No one seemed more excited than the Macklin wives. Grace, Amy, and Willow had volunteered to help Kell decorate the house. They'd take pictures and measurements Saturday morning, then leave for Missoula with a strict budget. The idea made Kell shudder.

While they were shopping, he and the brothers would be meeting with a contractor to remodel the existing barn and discuss a second one just inside the Macklin ranch. The original, smaller one would be used as a birthing barn between April and October, and the treatment of sick horses the other months of the year.

They were also considering building a modern day bunkhouse with six bedrooms, two baths, and kitchen. A firm decision hadn't been made, with Thorn and Del not sure it was needed, while Boone and Kell felt it worth pursuing. They planned to target equine majors at Montana State University, and local kids with an interest in horses. The near-term decision would come down to dollars.

His thoughts moved to Cliff, whose ankle had been improving each day, to the point he complained of being bored. A short-term solution had him running financial projections on the new barn, bunkhouse, and increased client base. If Cliff decided to stay in Whiskey Bend, there'd be plenty of opportunities at the ranch, or with one of the businesses in town.

Zane seemed content, although he'd been in talks with Del about a possible position as a deputy. He showed no interest in returning to his parents' farm. As Kell learned the hard way, plans could change with the beat of a heart.

Hearing his phone, he saw Boone's name. "What's up?"

"Larry wants to meet earlier. Does that work for you?"

"I'm just finishing. Meet you at the house in fifteen." Kell couldn't keep the smile from his face.

By the end of the day, his father's actions would be reversed, and he'd be the sole owner of the house, a barn, and three hundred acres.

Chapter Twenty-One

Beth stared out the window of the small diner near their office, waiting for Alana. Dark, foreboding thunderclouds were forming to the south, signaling the storm predicted earlier in the week. The weather didn't matter to her. She'd run in rain, light snow, and blistering heat, only balking if caught in a hailstorm.

The happenings of the last week had left her feeling oddly disconnected. Beth thought the new relationship with Kell had been going well. There'd been no pressure by either one, no demands, no drama. Seeing him with another woman had shaken her, made her wonder where she and Kell were headed. She hadn't had to wonder long.

Beth now faced a different future from the one in her head a week earlier. She hadn't expected a pronouncement of love or proposal of marriage. Her expectations weren't as life-altering. She'd envisioned an easy relationship with no demands placed on either of them. Beth didn't believe he walked away because of the nature of their relationship. Kell left because he didn't want her.

How could she fault him for making such a decision? She couldn't. Which meant Beth had to move on.

Leaving Whiskey Bend to attend law school became more definite with each passing week. Larry and Janet had been clear they wanted her to stay, but Beth could see just one way it would work.

People worked virtually all the time. It had become a common practice in many fields, why not in law? Because it shook up the predictable order. Law wasn't known for being innovative. Those in the field held expectations of how and where work was performed.

She also knew times were changing. Few people in the legal profession were as open to change as Larry and Janet. Perhaps they'd surprise her.

"Sorry you had to wait." Alana slung her purse over the back of the chair and sat down, flashing a brilliant smile. "Janet told me she and Larry have decided to change some of the processes and they want me to be involved."

"That's exciting. Do you have any idea what processes they're talking about?"

"Not yet. I'm open to anything more interesting than greeting clients and answering the phones. Don't get me wrong. I love my job, but it can get monotonous. Have you ordered?"

"I decided to wait for you. What's good here?"

"Everything. Their salads are spectacular. I've heard their sandwiches are the best in town. I always end up with a salad." Lowering her menu, Alana glanced toward the entrance. "Oh, no. Don't turn around, but Larry just came through the front door with Boone Macklin and Kell. I don't think they've seen us. I take that back. Larry lifted a hand in greeting, but isn't coming our way. You're in luck. They've picked a table across the room."

Beth inwardly groaned. The absolute last person she wanted to be anywhere close to was Kell.

Alana leaned toward her. "Do you want to go somewhere else?"

"Yes, but that would be too obvious. Let's order and ignore them." Beth had to get used to the idea of seeing Kell around town. It was one of the disadvantages of living in a small community where everyone knew everyone else.

"You have to like the eye candy. Kell is as handsome now as when we were in high school." The waitress sent a radiant smile toward the table across the room. "What will it be today, ladies?"

Both ordered a salad and tea, with Alana asking her to wrap three chocolate chip cookies to go. Waiting until the woman left, Alana leaned forward again.

"What do you know about Zane?"

Kell nursed his coffee while taking furtive glances across the room. Alana had spotted them the instant they entered the diner. No doubt she'd passed on what she saw to Beth, whose back was to the men.

She would've turned and waved a week ago, maybe come over to say hello. There'd be no acknowledgement today. He'd be lucky if she even met his gaze.

Kell vaguely heard Larry explain what they'd be signing. The closing date had been moved to today. A minor, yet important, change. The longer the sale dragged on, the higher the opportunity for problems.

Reaching for the paper Larry held out, he scribbled his name, passing it to Boone. They didn't need to meet in a diner to complete the signing. Kell wondered why they were here? Did Larry know about the relationship between him and Beth? Had he known she would be here?

Massaging the back of his neck, Kell knew he was being ridiculous. Larry wouldn't take time away from his busy practice to push two people together.

"I heard you and Beth are no longer seeing each other."

Kell's head whipped toward the attorney, eyes widening before he concealed his surprise. "How would you know that?"

"I have my ways, Kell. Beth is a valued employee. She's going to make an exceptional attorney one day. My hope is she'll choose to work for me and Janet right here in Whiskey Bend."

Kell lifted his cup, swallowing the cold coffee. "Probably best she find someone in law school. A man who matches her drive and intellect."

Leaning back in his chair, Larry draped an arm over the back. "You may be right. About the law school part. You make contacts for life while studying. Janet and I have attorney friends throughout the States and in foreign countries. They've been invaluable sources of information and referrals. My hope is Beth works as hard at building those contacts as at her studies. You need both to be successful." His attention moved from Kell to where Beth sat with Alana. "As for the rest, she's already met a man who matches her in drive and intellect."

Kell wanted to ask the man's name, fearing he already knew it.

Sitting up, Larry gathered up the papers, sliding them into a folder. Reaching across the table, he shook each of their hands.

"Congratulations on the purchase. And, Kell, I am glad you got your ranch back. Your father may have been a client, but he was never a friend."

As Larry walked out into the afternoon sun, a slack-jawed Kell watched him. He'd always believed his father and the attorney were tight. Believed Larry was instrumental in convincing his father to sell. He'd been wrong about all of it.

"You ready, Kell? I've got to get back to the ranch." Boone settled the Stetson on his head.

"Yeah." A slight grin lifted the corners of his mouth before he tugged Boone in for a bro-hug. "Thanks, man. I just, well...don't know what else to say."

Clasping Kell's shoulder, Boone shrugged as if his family's contribution wasn't a big deal. "It's a good investment. Your dad is a miserable human being. Always has been. I just wish we could've purchased the land when he decided to go against your agreement. We would've gladly worked out a deal with you."

Beth knew the instant Kell left the diner. She didn't turn around or try to get his attention. Nor did he try to get hers. Disappointment pressed down on her. She'd hoped he might come by to say hello, but, of course, he wouldn't. Their friendship of before had shifted to them being mere acquaintances.

"Are we still on for Wicked Waters tomorrow night?" Beth had no desire to sit alone at home. Between semesters, it would mean a glass of wine, dinner for one, and another of the movies she'd already seen a hundred times.

"Definitely. You should call Sarah Mae and have her join us. Both of you are men magnets."

"You don't need any help, Alana. Perhaps it's time to leave the past behind and move on."

Beth knew all about the death of her friend's fiancé eighteen months earlier. How he'd been in a car crash with his assistant as the passenger. It had happened late at night. Both had been dressed to go clubbing. The betrayal had changed Alana's view of men, as well as crushed her self-esteem.

"I know you're right, Beth. Every time I get up the nerve to accept an invitation to dinner, I wonder if I'm setting myself up for more hurt. Doug and I had been together for three years, with the wedding set a few weeks out. Why'd he ask me to marry him if he had his sights set on someone else?" Alana rubbed a spot on her temple.

"You may never know. I've had my share of losers, too. I may not be ready to get back into a relationship, but

I'm not going to let my breakup with Kell keep me at home. Who knows? Maybe there are fabulous men waiting in our future. We won't know if we don't get out there."

Beth cringed at the words streaming from her mouth. She'd never been a rah-rah type of girl, but if it took a pep talk to help Alana, that's what she'd get. Who knew? Along the way, perhaps some of the rah-rah would rub off on Beth.

"If you're ready to walk out, we can go together." Beth slung her purse over a shoulder, ready to call it a day.

"I'm ready. There's a hot bath and leftover lasagna waiting for me. There's plenty. You're welcome to join me."

Laughing, Beth pressed the elevator button. "The lasagna, yes. Not the bath."

They exited at the first floor, making their way to the back of the building to the parking area. The air outside held a comfortable warmth, common in early summer. Descending the three steps to the asphalt, a wave of cold stopped her.

"What's wrong?" Alana glanced around, seeing nothing to alarm her.

"I don't know. Something feels off." Making a slow turn of the almost deserted lot, she shrugged. "I'm sure it's nothing. I'll meet you at your place in an hour." They parted, each heading to their cars.

190

Climbing into her car, she set her purse aside, locked the door, and started the engine. Traffic was light both on the road and the sidewalks. Her apartment house had been built two blocks from downtown. She could walk, and probably should, but Beth liked having wheels if needed.

Pulling into the lot, she found a spot, grabbed her purse, and had just set both feet on the ground when a strong hand covered her mouth. There was no time to react before the other hand wrapped around her waist. Her assailant began tugging her toward the bushes lining the lot when Beth found the courage to react.

Plunging an elbow into his solar plexus, she had the satisfaction of hearing him grunt. His hold loosened enough for her to turn toward him, kicking him in the groin.

Believing him disabled, she twisted, meaning to run when his hand snaked out, snatching her ankle. One hard tug had her facedown on the asphalt. Unable to find anything to grab, she sucked in air and screamed.

Ear-piercing, she did it again as he dragged her over the asphalt. She could feel her clothes tearing, along with her skin. Flailing, she screamed again, although weaker than before.

Panic surged through her. Kicking with her free leg, she couldn't connect. If she didn't do something soon, her attacker would haul her into the bushes.

"Hey, you! Let her go!"

"Help! Help me!"

"Call the police."

"We have to help her!"

Several voices joined the first. She heard feet pounding on the pavement. More than one set. A group ran to help her.

Screaming once more, a fist landed hard to her stomach, silencing her voice and stealing the last amount of air from her lungs.

Chapter Twenty-Two

Del's jaw clenched. He'd arrived at the scene of an assault, never expecting the victim to be a woman he recognized.

Kneeling beside Beth, he brushed hair from her face while whispering her name. "That's it, Beth. Open your eyes for me."

Hearing sirens, he continued to comfort her. The neighbors, who chased the assailant away, brought blankets and water. He didn't dare lift her, not knowing the extent of her injuries.

"Beth. Can you hear me?"

She blinked several times, trying to keep her eyes open. When those efforts failed, she tried lifting her arm. A stinging sensation raced upward to her shoulder and down to the tips of her fingers.

Opening her mouth, her lips twisted before getting the whispered word out. "Del?"

"I'm here, Beth. Try to stay still. The EMTs are here. You're going to be fine." He hoped what he said was true. The injuries appeared painful, and would take time to heal, but not life- threatening. There could be internal injuries or broken ribs, though, and those concerned him.

Del stayed beside her while the professionals checked her vitals, and loaded her into the ambulance. He'd follow, and place a call to Amy. One deputy left that morning to attend a funeral in Billings, and another called in sick, forcing Del to take the night shift. Discovering Beth to be the victim, Del was glad he'd been the one at her side.

Pulling in beside the ambulance, he jumped out to walk beside the gurney. Her closed eyes gave the impression she slept. Then she blinked.

"Del?"

"I'm here, Beth. You'll be taken to emergency. If you have any concerns, ask a nurse to find me." He didn't tell her of his plan to call Kell.

Licking her lips, she formed two more words before being rolled into an examination cubicle. "Thank you."

Staying in the central area, he placed fisted hands on his hips, staring at the floor. Bruising had started around her eyes and one cheek. Asphalt abrasions covered her arms and legs, forehead, and to a lesser extent, her face.

Moving into the general waiting area, he walked outside, pulling out his phone. He had several calls to make. The first would be the hardest.

"Kell, it's Del. I'm at the hospital."

"Okay. Do you need something from me?"

"Beth was the victim of an assault."

"What? You could've started with that." Kell didn't try to hide his panic. "Who did it? Never mind, we can talk later. I'm on my way."

"They won't tell you anything. You know, the relative requirement. I'll stick around. The docs will talk to me."

"Thanks, Del. I'll see you in twenty."

Hanging up, the sheriff moved to the next call, hoping Larry Lawson would have information about Beth's family.

Tugging on boots, he grabbed his wallet, keys, and phone before hurrying down the stairs. Zane reclined in a large, leather chair, watching hockey reruns.

"Beth was attacked. She's in the hospital. I'm heading there now."

Zane's gaze moved from Kell's face to his hands, seeing them shake. He doubted his friend realized it. "You're not going alone. Hold on one minute and I'll drive."

"I can—"

Zane held up a hand, stopping whatever else Kell planned to say. "One minute. And you'd better still be here."

True to his word, Zane joined him outside. "We'll take my truck. You need time to get your shit together."

Sliding inside, Kell was about to object before he noticed his shaking hands. They never shook. Not during a mission, not when he'd heard about his father selling the ranch, and never over a woman. What was going on?

"Who did you talk to?"

Zane's question stopped Kell from digging too deep into the reasons for his body jumping out of his skin. "Del. He's at the hospital."

"Did he give you any other information? Extent of injuries, assailant, reason for the attack?"

Sucking in a breath, Kell swallowed the lump in his throat, giving a sharp shake of his head. "Nothing. I'll learn more after I've seen Beth."

"They may not let you see her."

"They will if I tell them I'm her fiancé."

Zane's mouth formed a small grin. "You're living dangerously. There's every reason to believe Beth will out you, man. You did dump her a week ago."

"She might, but not before I see her. One look is all I want." He needed to see her beautiful emerald eyes, even if they were filled with anger. Kell would figure out the rest one moment at a time.

Del met them at the front doors, nodding at both. "The doc treating her came out a few minutes ago. There's bruising on her face, arms, and ankle. According to witnesses, the assailant dragged her over the parking lot. There are asphalt burns on her arms, hands, legs, and some on her face. One cracked rib, but no internal injuries."

"Thank God," Kell breathed out.

"They're doing an MRI before moving her to a recovery room. Even if the MRI is clear, the doc said he'd have her stay overnight. Could've been a lot worse. She put up quite a fight. The neighbors heard her screams and ran the assailant off."

Kell thought of what the attacker might've done if he hadn't been scared off.

Zane cleared his throat. "Did you catch him?"

"No. I have a deputy interviewing witnesses."

"Just one?" Kell knew he had several.

"I'm short-staffed right now. He took off toward the parking lot on the other side of the row of bushes. A couple men followed. Saw him jump into a white truck. Neither got the license plate."

Zane took a quick look at the hospital lot. "There must be a thousand white trucks around Whiskey Bend."

"More than that. I'll have my other deputies back soon and put them on it. I'm hoping Beth will be able to give us a description. From what witnesses said, the man didn't wear a mask."

"Maybe one of them got a look at his face."

"Don't get your hopes up, Kell. From what I learned, it all happened fast. The neighbors weren't able to get close before the guy ran off. Joe Nolen is the deputy on scene taking statements. He won't let even the tiniest lead slip through the cracks." Del looked at Zane. They'd been talking about the former Special Forces soldier becoming a deputy. Del wanted him, but Zane needed time to consider the change.

"I could help you out until your other deputies return."

Del assessed him, wondering if Boone could do without Zane for a few days. "I'll speak with Boone. If he's good with it, then your help would be welcome."

"Fair enough."

Kell had stayed silent through Zane and Del's exchange, his mind locked on Beth. He needed to see her, assure himself she was going to be all right. And he wanted to know the results of the MRI. What came out of his mouth had nothing to do with either.

"Colonel August Hayward is behind the assault."

The other two shifted toward Kell, Del crossing his arms. "Why do you say that?"

"It's too coincidental. Beth was with me at the track. Olsen knows we're together. Rather, were together, but he doesn't know that."

"Olsen's in custody," Del said. "How could he get word to Hayward?"

"No clue, but I'm certain the colonel ordered the kidnapping. It may have been the reason Olsen was at the school." Kell's eyes flickered an instant, seeing a doctor walk toward them.

"Sheriff Macklin. Do you have a minute?"

"How is Beth?" Kell blurted out the question.

Adjusting his glasses, the doctor eyed him up and down "Are you a relative?"

"Her fiancé." Kell mentally thanked Del and Zane for not reacting.

"I see. Miss Hutchison has been moved to a room. We can discuss the MRI while we walk."

One hurdle down. A bigger one awaited him.

"I'm Doctor Allman." He held out his hand, which Kell shook.

"Kell Brooks."

"Miss Hutchison's MRI showed nothing of concern. Which doesn't mean she can go back to normal activities right away. I'd like to keep her overnight as a precautionary measure. She's already aware of this."

Touching the elevator button, Allman faced him. "Are you really her fiancé?"

Kell rocked back on his heels. "Hope to be soon."

"Ah. Well, I'll give you five minutes." Stopping outside her room, Allman's eyes twinkled. "Good luck, Mr. Brooks."

Chapter Twenty-Three

Kell stood outside the room, his hand damp on the knob. He could feel moisture on his brow, and an uncomfortable tightness in his chest. If he continued to stand in the hall, he might never talk to Beth.

Twisting the knob, he opened it an inch at a time. Her eyes were closed, chest rising and falling in an even rhythm.

Asleep. This might be for the best. She needed her rest, and he had some thinking to do before Beth woke up. Closing the door, he walked to the bed, his boots on the cushioned floor almost soundless.

Lifting a chair, he set it as close as he dared to the bed and sat down. Anger, hot and ferocious, lodged in his chest. The right side of her face was bruised, one eye swollen. On her left side, patches of gauze covered what he guessed was chafing from being dragged over the asphalt. The bruising was limited to a small area on the jaw.

His gaze moved to her right arm and hand, eliciting a curse. Lifting the sleeve of the gown, he could see more gauze bandages trailing from her shoulder to her wrist. A quick glance to her left arm revealed the same.

Closing his eyes, he took long, slow breaths in an attempt to temper his fury. Colonel Hayward had sent a man to do this to her. To hurt and kidnap Beth. Use her to gain Kell's silence.

Bending forward, he clasped his hands together, staring at the floor. He'd made an agreement with Zane and Cliff to stay out of the hunt and let the feds do their job. The promise became increasingly difficult.

Why hadn't they arrested Hayward? Why were they dragging this out, putting innocents in danger? With all they'd given them, and the rest of the evidence, the man should already be housed in a base stockade.

"Kell?" A hand touched his shoulder.

Straightening, he looked at her, features softening. "Hello, Beth. I hope it's all right I'm here."

She considered the comment, unable to bring herself to ask him to leave. "It's fine. I'm surprised they let you up here. You know. The requirement it be family."

Grimacing, he slid his palm under hers, his body reacting to her touch. "About that. I might've told the doctor I'm your fiancé."

He waited for a reaction, surprised when she laughed, then whimpered. "Ow. That hurts."

"What can I do?"

"Not make me laugh. It pulls the skin on my face. So you told them we're engaged?"

"Pretty much. I'm sorry, Beth, but I had to see you."

"I must look horrible."

"Considering what happened, you look damn fine." And she did. He shuddered, knowing it could've been so much worse.

"He caught me off guard. There were warning bells, but I didn't heed them. So stupid." She shifted under the covers, closing her eyes. "I'm so tired."

"Then sleep, sweetheart. I'll be right here."

One eye opened. "You will?"

"Unless the nurses kick me out, I'm not going anywhere."

A hand on his shoulder woke Kell. "Mr. Brooks. We need to take her vitals. Doctor Allman said you could stay in the room, but you'll need to move."

Scrubbing both hands over his face, he stood. "I'll be back in a few minutes."

He needed to use the restroom and locate a large cup of coffee. Checking the time, he saw it was four in the morning. Zane and Del wouldn't be downstairs, meaning Kell had no ride home. It didn't matter. Staying close to Beth had become his number one priority.

Colonel Hayward wouldn't be stupid enough to try and snatch her from the hospital. Yet he had sent someone to grab her from the parking lot of her own complex. Anywhere else and bystanders may not have jumped in to help.

Locating the cafeteria, he glanced around, hoping for something more than coffee. The lone cashier nodded toward a rack of crackers, cookies, and cupcakes. He picked up a package of chocolate chip cookies, and another of peanut butter crackers before filling a large cup with coffee.

Snatching a couple bottles of water, he paid. Again, he thought of Hayward, the task force, and the attack on Beth. Each angered him. Having been in the Army, Kell understood how slow the decision process could be.

Military operations were often expedited. Anything involving a task force could take months. Sometimes, years.

The first floor waiting area was empty. No smiling candy striper at the front desk or security guard inspecting those arriving and leaving. A perfect time of night to...

Punching the elevator button, he waited a moment before running to the stairs. Taking them two at a time, he reached the third floor, and rushed to her room. He stopped.

Beth was alone, asleep in the hospital bed. One nurse worked at her desk, looking up to smile at him. Nodding in return, he took a hard look up and down the hall before joining Beth.

She looked good. Even covered in bandages with a swollen eye and bruises, she was beautiful. His heart swelled. How had he walked away from her?

"You're an idiot, Brooks," he muttered, retaking his seat.

Tearing open the crackers, he finished the last one within minutes. Moving on to the cookies, he took a little more time, sipping coffee, forcing himself to relax. She was safe. There was no one stalking her. He'd allowed his imagination to control his actions.

What was happening to him? Considering the question, he knew. He'd fallen in love with Beth. A broken soldier had succumbed to the charms of a funny, smart, gorgeous woman.

Closing his eyes, he fell into a deep sleep.

"Kell. Wake up. We need to talk."

The voice ghosted through his brain. Fighting it, he slipped back into the comfortable world of sleep.

"Kell. I have information you need." This time, he felt his body rock.

Blinking several times, he forced his eyes open. Del stood in front of him. His gaze moved to Beth, who still slept.

"What is it?" His voice sounded as if he'd swallowed a bucket of sand. He checked the time. Nine in the morning. Kell had slept through at least one pass by the nurse.

A cup of coffee appeared. He took it with a grateful nod, taking several swallows.

"We found the man who attacked Beth."

Choking, he set the cup aside. "Let's go into the hall."

Flinching at his stiff muscles, he pushed up, stretching before following Del.

"Joe was called to the scene of an accident on the county road to Missoula. A motorist reported a white truck had driven off the road. The driver was unconscious in the front seat. The airbag deployed, but there was still a long gash on his forehead. The EMTs arrived and loaded him up. That's when Joe ran the driver's license. The guy is an Army major. We did a deeper search and found he's based at Fort Lewis. Guess who his commanding officer is?"

"Hayward," Kell growled.

"Right. It took a while, but I located the number for Colonel Hayward."

"And?"

"He's missing. Left the base yesterday morning and hasn't been back. His wife and children aren't home. The neighbors haven't seen them in at least a week."

Kell blew out a vulgar curse. "They left the country."

"That's my guess. Base security thinks they may have been taken."

"Bull. The man sent his family away, then followed when it was safe. Did they find anything in his office?"

"No." Reaching into his jacket, he pulled out a small, leather journal. "This was delivered to me an hour ago. FedEx. Signature required. I read the first ten pages and the last ten. You were right about him, Kell."

He took the journal from Del's hand. "Do Rhodes and Swallow know about it?"

"Not yet. I thought you'd want to read it first. We should make a couple copies before handing it over to the feds. Go through it. I'll stay with Beth."

The nurse directed Kell to a small lounge on the same floor. Closing the door, he began to read.

An hour past before he finished the last page, ready to hunt down Hayward and choke the life from him. The man played an integral role in spreading drugs throughout the northwest. He poisoned men, women, and children with the drugs he put on the streets.

The journal detailed how he'd been able to ship the drugs from Afghanistan on military transports, bringing the packages to Fort Lewis. The drugs were moved off the base, passed to the cartel for distribution at dozens of locations in Washington, Idaho, and Montana.

So many lives ruined because of a decorated Army colonel who'd turned traitor. For money. Lots and lots of it. Enough to establish him and his family in a different country with new identifies. Kell hoped the man choked on his wealth.

Closing the journal, he returned to Beth's room, still stunned by what Hayward had written. If he were still a Ranger, he'd use all the intel at his disposal, find the man who'd murdered his brothers, and neutralize him.

But he was no longer in the Army, had no access to the intel required to find a man hiding in a country without an extradition treaty with the United States. Kell had to settle for satisfaction knowing Hayward could no longer transport drugs into the country.

"Here you go." Kell handed the journal back to Del. "You're right about making copies. The information is explosive. Do you think Hayward sent a copy to the task force?"

"I don't know. I'll get it to Rhodes tomorrow, then it will be his problem. Beth woke up for about twenty minutes when the nurse came in. She said the doctor will be by this morning to determine if she can go home. You know she won't be able to be by herself for a while. Talk to Boone about taking her to the ranch."

Pinching the bridge of his nose, Kell shook his head. "I can't add one more burden to your brother and Willow. He also needs me to get back to work. I'm thinking of hiring someone to stay with Beth at her place until she can return to work."

Del looked at him as if he'd gone loco. "Forget it. If you want to get her back, take her to the ranch. She needs to know how much you want her. That won't happen if you dump her at the apartment." He clasped Kell on the shoulder. "You can still hire someone to watch her while you work."

Watching Del stroll out of the room, Kell let the idea settle in his head. Before going back into her room, he punched in a number on his phone.

"This is Kell Brooks. I need someone to stay with a recovering patient at my ranch. Starting tomorrow."

Chapter Twenty-Four

"I want to go home." Beth's condition, and voice, had improved ten-fold since the night before. Her disposition was another matter.

"You are going home. It just happens to be my place and not your apartment."

Waving an arm in the air, she winced at the shot of pain. "That's ridiculous. You'd have to move clothes, the vitamins I take, my laptop..." She shook her head. "Too much to make sense."

"Already done."

Her voice rose to a shriek. "Who gave you permission to enter my apartment?"

Smirking, he sat on the edge of the bed. "I'm your fiancé, remember? The manager let me inside when he learned what I needed." Reaching out, he stroked a finger down the less injured cheek, chuckling when she moved away. "I can be quite persuasive when needed."

"You should've told me, Kell. Better yet, you should've asked." Touching her temple, she closed her eyes. "I have a headache."

"I'll call the nurse."

"Don't. I don't want to take more meds. Do you want to know what I want?"

"I'm sure you'll tell me."

Closing her eyes, she sighed. "A bath."

"Sorry, sweetheart, but that's not going to work. Until those bandages are removed, you'll have to settle for a warm, soapy washcloth. I'll be happy to help you."

Reaching for the cup of water, she drew several sips through the straw. "Why are you doing this, Kell? You ended us a week ago." She sucked more water through the straw, looking away. "It would be easier for both of us if you take me home."

The cocky grin he'd sported earlier had disappeared. Kell hadn't considered the hurt he'd caused Beth.

"I'm sorry. I never meant to hurt you."

"You would've done the same even if you'd realized how it would hurt me. I saw it on your face. In your eyes. I had become a problem to deal with." A mirthless chuckle escaped her lips. "I don't blame you, Kell. But if it's all the same to you, I'd rather not go through it again. Let me go home. It's for the best."

Two weeks later...

"Glad you're back where you belong, Beth. We've missed you." Larry rested a hip against the edge of his desk. "How do you feel?"

"Good. Excellent, in fact. Ready to get back to work." *And away from Kell.*

He'd checked on her every day, leaving her inside the apartment. A bag filled with dinner from Doc's, the bistro, or another restaurant would be clutched in one hand, her favorite orange soda in the other.

"Alana told me you hired a temp while I was gone. I could've done the work from home."

"Janet mentioned the idea, but I vetoed it. You needed to rest and heal, Beth. The young man was competent and professional. We're discussing adding him to the staff as your assistant."

"My assistant? Is there that much work?"

"Since you've been gone, the firm has added three new clients. One is a tech company relocating from the outskirts of Missoula. Thirty employees are moving to Whiskey Bend. The other fifteen will work virtually, driving to the new offices one day a week. The company is saving tens of thousands, and the employees are happy with the change. So, yes. The work has grown considerably."

"Welcome back, Beth. Has Larry told you about the young man we want to hire as your assistant?"

"Good morning, Janet. He was just explaining the reasons for hiring him."

"You're an excellent paralegal, Beth, and you're good with people. Thomas is a fast learner and willing to listen. He'll make a more than competent legal assistant. I believe the two of you will work well together."

"When do I get to meet him?"

"Next Monday is his first day. I'd suggest you take some time to list which duties you'll assign him. Glad you're here, Beth." Janet touched Larry's arm, smiling before leaving for her office.

Larry followed his wife and business partner. Beth watched, a seed of jealousy lodging in her throat. She wanted what her bosses and the Macklin brothers had.

The love flowing between husbands and wives, the devotion to each so obvious, it made her heart ache. Most knew Beth had a goal to attend law school, leading to a career as an attorney. Few knew how much she craved a man who'd love and cherish her. A man who wanted it all—marriage, a house, and family.

In a short few weeks, she'd fallen for Kell, believing he might be interested in a relationship beyond Friday night dinners and great sex. He hadn't.

She owed him for being there during her stay in the hospital and the recovery period at home. Kell had hired and paid for the home care nurse, stopped by her apartment each day, bringing dinner in a bag. He cared about her, but didn't want anything more. He didn't want *her*.

"Hey, stranger." Alana leaned down, giving her a gentle hug. "Are you glad to be back with us?"

"More than you know. Stuck at home for two weeks isn't as fun as it sounds. What about you?"

"Same as usual. Nothing new. Well, except for Thomas."

"Larry and Janet told me they've hired him to work as my assistant. What are your thoughts?"

Glancing behind her at the partners' offices, she tapped a finger against her lips. "He's still learning. The resume listed two years' experience as an assistant in a Missoula accounting office. Nothing in law. He does seem to be a quick learner. And he's kind of cute in a geek sort of way."

A sharp laugh burst from Beth on the last. "Guess I'll see for myself."

"Did Kell continue to bring dinner to you every night? I mean, all except the night I came over. So, did he?"

"Yes, but don't make more of it than a friend stopping by. He has no interest in me other than possibly a friend."

"Oh."

"It's for the best. At least I didn't have to wait months to find out I'm not what he wants. Kell is a good man and I wish him the best. We're just not meant to be together." Beth picked up a file, then dropped it on her desk. "I'd better get started on this stack of work. Do you want to meet for lunch?"

"That'd be great. Glad you're back."

Kell studied the plans for the new barn, asking a few questions before giving his approval. The three Macklins had already given their okay on it and the changes to the birthing barn. The former would be built on the border between the two ranches, while the birthing barn already existed on Kell's acreage. The plans for remodeling it included everything on the list they'd provided the builder.

"It's great. When can you start?"

"I had another client reschedule, which opened up my calendar. We can start tomorrow."

"Sounds great. What do you need from us?"

"A signature. You're the last to sign the contract. Plus I'll need thirty percent down for supplies."

Writing a check from the partnership account, satisfaction wrapped around him. The wives had finished with their work on the interior of his house, the builder's crew had laid out the perimeter of the new barn, and remodeling the birthing barn would begin tomorrow.

All was good in his life. Except for one thing. Beth thought he didn't want her, and it was his fault. He'd done a poor job explaining what he'd meant a few weeks earlier. There wasn't much he regretted in his life. That night was one of them.

What he'd said about taking a break was accurate. Beth had taken it not as a cooling off period, but as an ending. Kell needed time to sort out his feelings before he did anything to hurt her. Turned out, he'd hurt her anyway.

Starting tonight, things were about to change.

Parking in the lot of her complex, Beth sat there, hands shaking. Her chest felt tight, her breathing erratic.

Glancing out the windows, she took a look in the rearview mirror. Was the shadow a person or a play of lights? Beth couldn't be sure.

Kell had told her the man who'd attacked her had been arrested. He'd been identified as a major in the Army, and now sat in the base stockade, awaiting trial.

What if he'd escaped, waiting for her to leave the safety of her car?

Her body jerked at the knock on the driver's window. She forced herself to look to her left, expecting a man wearing a ski mask. Instead, Kell stood outside.

"Are you all right, Beth?"

Releasing a shaky breath, she lowered her head an instant before returning her gaze to his. Unlocking the door, she climbed outside.

His hands settled on her shoulders, sensing the tension. "It's all right, Beth. There's no threat. Nobody waiting to attack you."

"Sorry. I'm not usually like this."

"You're allowed." Tugging her closer, he wrapped her in his arms. Moving his hand up and down her back, he rested his chin on the top of her head. "The attack was brutal. It'll take a while for you to be comfortable with basic activities. Such as parking. Don't see it as bad. The attack will make you more aware of your surroundings. Where are your keys?"

Leaning back, she held the ring between her and Kell. Taking them, he reached inside to grab her purse, then locked the door.

"Come on. Let's get to your apartment."

Beth looked into his face. "I'm fine now, Kell. Don't feel you have to stay."

"This is exactly where I want to be." His meaningful gaze locked with hers before turning them toward the walkway.

Entering her apartment, she tossed her purse on the sofa, heading straight for the kitchen. "I'm going to make tea. Do you want some?"

"You take care of the tea while I make coffee."

They worked in silence, her setting the teapot aside to steep before turning to face him. "Why are you here, Kell?"

He offered a slight smile. "Habit?"

"That's not it."

Picking up his cup, Kell blew across the top. "No, it isn't." Swallowing some of the hot liquid, he lowered the cup. "I wanted to see you, Beth. What happened a few weeks ago..." He inhaled a slow breath. "I never should've walked away from you."

Chapter Twenty-Five

Beth's mouth dropped open for several seconds as she stared at him. Disbelief, confusion, and distrust warred for a place in her head. This had to be a joke. Didn't it?

Kell's words would've had her shouting with joy a month ago. She loved him. Or she had until he destroyed her hopes with a few words and unyielding expression. That was a lie. Beth still loved him, would for a long time.

She'd finally accepted they had no future together, learned to deal with the emptiness and pain. Now this.

"I've regretted my words and actions ever since." Kell took a step closer, stopping at the wariness on her face.

Taking an involuntary step back, she crossed her arms. "What, exactly, are you trying to say?"

"I want another chance, Beth."

She shook her head, not believing what he'd said. "So you can break my heart a second time? No. I was a fool once. I won't go through it again."

He held out his hands. "It was never my intention to hurt you, Beth. Even though I'd done nothing wrong, guilt punched me in the gut when you walked into Wicked Waters and found me with someone else. I saw the flash of pain on your face. That's when I realized your feelings for me ran deep. I wasn't ready to deal with defining our relationship or where it might be going."

"If you weren't ready to talk, why did you come to my apartment?"

Kell massaged the back of his neck, recalling that night. "I shouldn't have come here. In hindsight, I should've finished the evening and gone home. Given both of us time to calm down."

Pouring a cup of tea, Beth walked into the living room, taking a seat at one end of the sofa. "But you didn't."

Lowering himself into a nearby chair, he leaned forward, resting his arms on his thighs. "No, I didn't."

She brushed hair out of her eyes. "Did I say something to trigger your leaving? Push too hard about being with someone else?" Kell gave a slow shake of his head. "I must've done something."

"None of what happened that night was your fault, Beth." Glancing away, his gaze moved around the room where he'd spent so much time. Where he'd felt so much.

"As we talked, it became clear I was in too deep. I had feelings for you, Beth, but wasn't prepared to accept them. I didn't want to be boxed into a relationship so soon. One I didn't understand, with a woman I'd known only a few weeks."

She sipped her tea, understanding what he was trying to say. Beth had thought the same until accepting she loved him.

"I've had a lot of time to think since that night. I miss you, Beth. More than I thought possible." Standing, he moved to sit beside her on the sofa. Taking one of her hands in his, he leaned closer. "I love you, Beth. Give me a second chance to prove it."

Heart pounding a painful rhythm, she looked down at their joined hands. She thought of that night, the pain his leaving caused. The last few weeks, Beth had told herself over and over she no longer loved Kell, was over him. It was a lie.

How would she survive if they tried again with the same result? She'd never seen herself as a coward, yet the decision facing her made Beth consider running.

"Can I have time to think about it, Kell?"

He visibly relaxed. At least it wasn't a no. "As much time as you need. For tonight, I want to take you to dinner. Any restaurant you want."

"If you're sure."

"I am. Where would you like to go?"

Zane held the post steady while Kell poured rapid-setting cement over six inches of pea gravel in the bottom of the hole. Fifteen minutes later, the two men loaded the supplies in the back of Kell's truck.

By the time they reached his house, Beth would be there to see the changes inside. Four weeks had passed since their discussion at her apartment. Neither had brought up his request. He'd promised to give her all the time she needed, and Kell was determined to keep his word.

He'd met her for lunch, taken her to dinner, and driven to Missoula to see a movie over the last month. Kell doubted they'd see each other any more often if she had agreed to a second chance.

"Is that her SUV?" Zane nodded toward the front of the house.

A broad smile appeared on Kell's face. "That's hers."

Parking next to the barn, he climbed out, waving to where Beth sat in a rocker on the porch. Taking the steps two at a time, he pulled her up and into his arms.

"Okay if I kiss you?" He'd asked each time they were together, not wanting to push her too fast. She'd always said yes, leaning into him as if she belonged there.

"I'd be worried if you didn't."

Bending down, he captured her mouth, deepening the kiss while running his hands up and down her back. He wanted to sweep her into his arms and carry her inside to his new bed. Until she gave him her decision, he wouldn't do anything to jeopardize their tenuous connection.

Before he did what he wanted instead of what he should, Kell ended the kiss. Staring into glassy, deep green eyes, he saw so much more than a beautiful woman who warmed his heart.

Dismissing the rest before he jinxed what he hoped to be a future with Beth, he took her hand, leading her inside. Starting with the downstairs, he showed her each room.

"You said Grace, Amy, and Willow did all this for you?"

"They sure did. We met for about an hour to talk about colors and other stuff before they went shopping in

Missoula. Some of the furniture was stored here in town. The rest is new. All except the kitchen. The women shopped thrift stores for that room. The dishes and cooking pans are new, but the rest is used. They saved me a ton of money."

Beth listened to all the women had accomplished, a wisp of jealousy tightening her throat. She'd hoped Kell would've asked her to help.

"Did they do most of this while I laid up?"

Hearing something in her voice, Kell lifted her chin with a finger. "Pretty much. I was anxious to move in, so it all happened fast. There are four bedrooms upstairs. Two haven't been touched. Would you want to help me with those?"

"I'd love to." Her smile lit his world.

Returning her smile, he tightened his hold on her hand. "Let me show you the upstairs."

Showing her the two empty bedrooms first, they moved to furnished ones, ending with the master suite. The biggest of the bedrooms with its own bath, the women had furnished it in masculine colors.

"The bed frame, tables, and dresser were in storage. Mom used them in one of the guest bedrooms. She and my father didn't want to move them to Florida. They sold the furniture in my bedroom." The last was said with unmistakable sadness.

Placing her hand on his arm, she looked up at him. "The room is beautiful, Kell, as is the rest of the house. I'm so happy for you. What your parents did wasn't right. But their actions gave you a chance to build a future on your terms. The future you want."

Rising on her toes, she brushed a kiss across his mouth before doing it once more, this time lingering. Kell's arms wrapped around her, the kiss intense and probing.

His hands roamed over her back, one finding its way under her blouse to the clasp of her bra. He wanted to make love to her, feel her heated skin, let her know how much he craved her.

Beth's soft moan should've spurred him on, had him removing her bra to cup her luscious breasts. Instead, the sound stilled his hands. Until she made a decision about them, he'd wait. Kell had made a promise to himself, and he meant to keep it.

Shoving aside the intense passion, he slipped his hand from under her blouse, ended the kiss, and stepped away.

"What's wrong?" Beth's glazed eyes crinkled at the corners in confusion.

"Nothing, sweetheart."

"Then, why did you stop?"

Taking her hand, he led her to the edge of the bed. "Sit down, Beth."

"But..."

"Please."

Pursing her lips, she did as he asked. Holding both hands in his, Kell knelt in front of her.

"I believe my feelings for you are clear. I love you, and that won't change. You needed time to make a decision about us. A decision to give me a second chance or move on."

Brows drawing together, she moistened her lips. "You said I could take as much time as needed."

"And you can. I'll spend as much time with you as possible until you make up your mind. While you're deciding, I don't think it's a good idea to make love. If you decide to move on, it would make the break that much harder. When and if we make love, I need to know we're both looking for the same outcome. A future together."

Beth considered his words, showing no anger or frustration. She understood his need to know where she stood. He'd been honest about his feelings, his desire for a future.

She did love him. Her hesitancy had come from fear Kell would walk away a second time. The last few weeks had convinced her the mistake he made before wouldn't be repeated. When Kell opened his mouth to speak again, she placed a finger over his lips.

"You're right. Making love would make it more difficult to walk away." She replaced her finger with her hand, cupping his cheek. "I love you, Kell. Have for most of the time I've known you. I do want a second chance." She pressed a soft kiss to his mouth before leaning away.

A small smile lifted the corners of his mouth at the same time his hand reached into a pocket. Holding the object in his hand, he met her gaze.

"The second chance I envision is a commitment, Beth. We love each other. I want to honor this love with a pledge. Bethany Hutchison, you're the woman of my dreams. You're my friend, my lover, the person I want to see when falling asleep and waking in the morning. A future without you is unimaginable. Marry me, Beth. Marry me and make this second chance our future."

She couldn't stop the tears from escaping or the squeal of surprise. "Are you certain, Kell? Really, truly certain I'm what you want?"

"I've never been more sure of anything in my life. You're it for me, Beth. Be my wife."

She stared at him so long he thought she might not answer. When she opened her mouth, his fears she'd turn him down fled.

"I love you, Kellen Brooks. I'd be honored to be your wife." Wrapping her arms around his neck, she kissed him, long and deep, with all the love she felt.

When he pulled away, opening his palm, her eyes widened. "It's...it's..."

"For you, Beth." Taking her hand, he slipped it on her finger. "To our future."

Through tear-filled eyes, she nodded. "To our future."

Epilogue

Three months later...

Kell fumbled with the buttons on his vest, unable to get a single one through its hole. He had three minutes before heading downstairs to stand by the men who'd become his family.

"Looks like you could use some help." Boone walked through the bedroom door, stopping in front of him. With an ease Kell couldn't summon, Boone slipped the buttons in place and stepped back. "What else?"

"Just my jacket." He looked down at his polished boots before reaching up to touch the brim of his cowboy hat.

Boone held up his jacket, waiting as Kell slid his arms inside. Running his hands down the fabric to smooth the wrinkles, he smiled.

"Damn. You do clean up well, brother." Drawing Kell into a quick bro-hug, Boone headed for the door. "Time to meet your fate. Don't worry. If you faint, I'll make sure you don't wrinkle the fine clothing."

Chuckling, Kell followed Boone down the stairs to take his place beside the Macklin brothers and Zane. Looking out at the small crowd gathered in his living room, he thought of his decision to not invite his parents. Kell had no regrets about the choice. After the honeymoon, he'd send a picture with Beth's name.

His gaze locked on Larry Lawson, a man who'd done so much to get the ranch back in Kell's hands. Giving the older man an appreciative nod, his throat tightened. Behind Larry sat several men who'd been squad members, his brothers in arms. Cliff or Zane must've gotten the word out.

Seeing those men, he fought a tear. No way he'd let them see how much their being there meant to him. At least not with tears. He'd never hear the end of it.

The soft music background faded away as the Wedding March began. Lifting his head, he sucked in a breath at the sight of Beth standing just inside the front door. Her parents had arrived from Billings two days earlier. With her father beside her, Beth walked toward him. Her smile was radiant and directed straight at him.

Minutes passed in a blur. Kell heard the minister and answered as expected. Before he knew it, the minister said he could kiss his bride. He did it with flair, bending her over his arm for a deep kiss.

The small crowd applauded, his former team members hooted and whistled. Ending the kiss, he took her hand, mouthing *I love you* before walking down the short aisle.

Never in his life did he think the painful runs around the high school track would lead to finding the love of his life. Looking around, Kell realized how blessed he was.

Three years ago, he faced a bleak future. The ranch had been sold, he'd left the Army with a medical discharge, and he faced months of physical therapy.

"Are you all right?" Beth smiled up at her husband.

Kissing her, he returned her bright smile. "I can't imagine my life being any better. I love you, Beth."

"And I love you, Kell." Squeezing his hand, she looked over the crowd, her gaze landing on the table filled with buffet items. At one end sat a three layer cake. She felt her stomach growl. "Let's move this party along, handsome. I'm ready for cake."

Laughing, she tugged him toward the table near the kitchen, and a future he couldn't wait to start.

Learn about upcoming books in the Macklins of Whiskey Bend series.

Enjoy the Macklin brothers? Here's another series you might want to read. MacLarens of Fire Mountain Contemporary Western Romance series.

If you want to keep current on all my preorders, new releases, and other happenings, sign up for my newsletter at: http://www.shirleendavies.com/contact-me.html

A Note from Shirleen

Thank you for taking the time to read **Boone**!

If you enjoyed it, please consider telling your friends or posting a short review. Word of mouth is an author's best friend and much appreciated.

I care about quality, so if you find something in error, please contact me via email at shirleen@shirleendavies.com

Books by Shirleen Davies

Contemporary Western Romance Series

MacLarens of Fire Mountain

Second Summer, Book One
Hard Landing, Book Two
One More Day, Book Three
All Your Nights, Book Four
Always Love You, Book Five
Hearts Don't Lie, Book Six
No Getting Over You, Book Seven
'Til the Sun Comes Up, Book Eight
Foolish Heart, Book Nine

Macklins of Whiskey Bend

Thorn, Book One
Del, Book Two
Boone, Book Three
Kell, Book four

Historical Western Romance Series

Redemption Mountain

Redemption's Edge, Book One
Wildfire Creek, Book Two
Sunrise Ridge, Book Three
Dixie Moon, Book Four
Survivor Pass, Book Five
Promise Trail, Book Six
Deep River, Book Seven
Courage Canyon, Book Eight
Forsaken Falls, Book Nine
Solitude Gorge, Book Ten
Rogue Rapids, Book Eleven
Angel Peak, Book Twelve
Restless Wind, Book Thirteen
Storm Summit, Book Fourteen
Mystery Mesa, Book Fifteen
Thunder Valley, Book Sixteen
A Very Splendor Christmas, Holiday Novella, Book
Seventeen
Paradise Point, Book Eighteen,
Silent Sunset, Book Nineteen
Rocky Basin, Book Twenty
Captive Dawn, Book Twenty-One, Coming Next in the
Series!

MacLarens of Fire Mountain

Tougher than the Rest, Book One
Faster than the Rest, Book Two
Harder than the Rest, Book Three
Stronger than the Rest, Book Four
Deadlier than the Rest, Book Five
Wilder than the Rest, Book Six

MacLarens of Boundary Mountain

Colin's Quest, Book One,
Brodie's Gamble, Book Two
Quinn's Honor, Book Three
Sam's Legacy, Book Four
Heather's Choice, Book Five
Nate's Destiny, Book Six
Blaine's Wager, Book Seven
Fletcher's Pride, Book Eight
Bay's Desire, Book Nine
Cam's Hope, Book Ten

Romantic Suspense

Eternal Brethren, Military Romantic Suspense

Steadfast, Book One
Shattered, Book Two
Haunted, Book Three
Untamed, Book Four

Devoted, Book Five
Faithful, Book Six
Exposed, Book Seven
Undaunted, Book Eight
Resolute, Book Nine
Unspoken, Book Ten
Defiant, Book Eleven
Consumed, Book Twelve, Coming Next in the Series!

Peregrine Bay, Romantic Suspense

Reclaiming Love, Book One
Our Kind of Love, Book Two
Edge of Love, Book Three, Coming Next in the Series!

Find all of my books at:
https://www.shirleendavies.com/books.html

About Shirleen

Shirleen Davies writes romance—historical, contemporary, and romantic suspense. She grew up in Southern California, attended Oregon State University, and has degrees from San Diego State University and the University of Maryland. Her real passion is writing emotionally charged stories of flawed people who find redemption through love and acceptance. She now lives with her husband in a beautiful town in northern Arizona.

I love to hear from my readers!

Send me an email: shirleen@shirleendavies.com
Visit my Website: https://www.shirleendavies.com/
Sign up to be notified of New Releases:
https://www.shirleendavies.com/contact/
Follow me on Amazon:
http://www.amazon.com/author/shirleendavies
Follow me on BookBub:
https://www.bookbub.com/authors/shirleen-davies

Other ways to connect with me:

Facebook Author Page:
http://www.facebook.com/shirleendaviesauthor
Pinterest: http://pinterest.com/shirleendavies
Instagram:
https://www.instagram.com/shirleendavies_author/
TikTok: shirleendavies_author
Twitter: www.twitter.com/shirleendavies